I dumped her on the bed and started peeling her clothes off. I stripped off her coat, the pants of her pantsuit, the panties, bra, stockings, and shoes. When she was naked I picked them up and dropped them on a chair in a pile. She jumped up and darted for them. I grabbed her, held her, and began undressing myself. One-handed, it was a job, but it didn't take long. When I was naked, too, I pulled the spread back. Then I rolled her in and climbed in beside her. At last, when I held her to me, her mouth found mine, and from there on in, it was volcanic.

THE INSTITUTE

James M. Cain

LEISURE BOOKS ❧ **NEW YORK CITY**

A LEISURE BOOK

Published by

Nordon Publications, Inc.
Two Park Avenue
New York, N.Y. 10016

Copyright© MCMLXXVI by James M. Cain

THE
INSTITUTE

I first met Hortense Garrett at her home in Wilmington, Delaware on a spring morning last year. I wasn't calling on her but on her husband, Richard Garrett, the financier, to make a pitch for money—a lot of money, twenty million or so. It was for a project I had in mind, an institute of biography which I hoped he would endow—and, incidentally, name me as director.

Promptly at ten, as my appointment called for, I went up to the top deck of the Newcastle Arms, the apartment house where he lived, first by express to the fifteenth floor and then in a private elevator to the twentieth. I rang the bell marked GARRETT and was let in by a Swedish maid who first asked my name through a peephole. After taking my hat and coat she showed me into the living room—or drawing room, I suppose one would call it, that was big going on gigantic.

"I tell Mr. Garrett you here," she said and left, while I started looking around. And there was plenty to look at. First, there was a view of the Delaware River and what looked like half the state of New Jersey, which was nothing short of breathtaking. Next, there were furnishings of an unusual kind: a big, rich, overstuffed sofa and chairs, all in a uniform light beige; tables, cabinets, and knickknacks in dark mahogany; and two oriental rugs placed edge to edge, which carpeted the floor comfortably, yet left some hardwood showing. Around the walls were pictures, all by the same artist, apparently. There were woodland scenes with streams running through and sunlit roads with trees shading them.

It was overwhelming, yet at the same time homelike, perhaps because of the sentimental look of the pictures. But in the midst of my tour of inspection, this girl came whirling into the room with her hand outstretched. She was in her midtwenties, medium-sized but verging on small, with nice contours. Her features, though stubby, had shadows high on the cheeks. Her hair was a tawny blonde, about the color of cornhusks, and her eyes had an odd way of looking at me, sort of half-closed. She was wearing a bottle-green pantsuit that helped the green of her eyes, with a blouse under the jacket that was pulled slightly tight in front.

"Dr. Palmer," she announced, "I'm Mrs. Garrett. My husband will be with you directly. He apologizes for making you wait, but a call just came in from Paris and he felt he should take it."

I was taken by surprise. *Who's Who in America* gave his age as forty-one, and though it mentioned his marriage, I wasn't prepared for a girl who looked even younger than I was, which was twenty-eight at the time.

I took her hand and said: "Mrs. Garrett, if it means the delight of your company, I hope his call goes on and on and on."

8

"That's a very pretty speech."

"To a very pretty girl."

We both laughed, then she asked how well I knew Senator Hood of Nebraska who had introduced me over the phone and set up my appointment with Mr. Garrett.

"Not very well," I said, "but a lot better than casually. I was able to help him once when his boy got in trouble with the law, and a senator never forgets. Also, a senator's wife is not indifferent to a young man with a dinner jacket."

"Oh my, God's perfect gift to the hostess."

To change the subject, I asked who the artist was.

"Wallace Nutting. A friend of my husband's father. They're nice watercolors but no better than that, really. Nutting was the greatest furniture-maker this country ever produced, though—or at least, so my husband thinks." She waved toward the mahogany things, which even I could see were quite special.

Mrs. Garrett motioned me to a seat on one of the sofas facing the fireplace and took her place on the other, facing me. The way she sat highlighted her blouse and what was inside it, so I only half-paid attention as she resumed talking about Senator Hood and how close her husband and the senator were.

Suddenly Mr. Garrett walked into the room, apologizing for keeping me waiting. He was tall, almost as tall as I am, which is six-feet-one, gray-haired and rawboned. He had on a sweatshirt and slacks. His eyes were a watery gray, his voice a toneless drone. And yet his manner was friendly enough, even more than had been necessary in order to comply with protocol for seeing a young college professor who had been introduced by a United States senator.

Mr. Garrett explained that he had to take the call from Paris, "on account of the time differential—they stay up all night to call at an hour that's convenient for me, so I can't just give them the brush." He kept looking at me, then suddenly asked: "Dr. Palmer, have we met before?"

"Well . . . have we, Mr. Garrett?" To say "not as I recall" wouldn't have been very friendly, but to fake something would have been worse. I couldn't recall ever having laid eyes on him, though. Mr. Garrett shot another couple of glances at me. Months later, it became clear where and how I had met him, why he had remembered and I had not; but for now he cut it off and switched to what I'd come about. "An institute of biography, the senator said. I'll admit, just hearing that much about it, I'm intrigued. So let's have the details." When he had sat down beside his wife on the sofa and I had resumed my seat, he continued: "I've asked my wife to join us because in a matter like this, it shouldn't be my decision alone. Unless she shares my enthusiasm, I won't undertake it."

"I'm sure I'm going to."

We all laughed, and he motioned for me to get going. So I gave it the works. I talked about the American preeminence in biography, waving the flag quite a lot as he began to nod his head. I mentioned the strange academic indifference to it, "there being no courses in it as, at least as far as I know. It's not what's called a *discipline* anywhere." Warming to the subject, I spoke of the various ways an institute could help the biographer, "for example, by claiming a half-dozen study rooms in Archives and the Library of Congress."

"You'd be based in Washington, then?"

"I would think so, yes."

"Just wanted to know. Go on."

"We could assign those rooms ourselves without going through the bureaucratic rigamarole, one of the nuisances a writer runs into nowadays." I mentioned the microfilm room I thought we should have, "with a battery of Recordak readers available at all times." He seemed to know about these and nodded. "Also," I said, "and quite importantly, we'd maintain a taping studio on the order of the Department of Oral History that Allen Nevins started at Columbia, where our writers could put their subjects on some kind of permanent record. And I think we should provide genealogy researchers to ease that kinky angle all biographers dread and yet can't sidestep—what a lift that would be."

"What about cash grants?"

"Oh, grants-in-aid will be necessary. In fact, they will be desperately needed. You have no idea how expensive biography is."

He got up, found a clipboard in the escritoire, stuck some paper in it, and began taking notes with a ballpoint pen. He studied them as I sat across from him, watching. I had the excited feeling that I had scored.

"Dear?" he asked his wife. "What do you think? Does it interest you at all?"

"Oh definitely. . . . Yes, it thrills me."

That's what she said, but it had a phoney ring; and if I noticed it, so did he. He studied her for a moment and then growled: "Well? What don't you like about it?"

"But I *do* like it, Richard," she exclaimed. "I think it's wonderful. And I know, myself, that they don't have the courses in it. You forget, dear; I was a teach-

11

ing assistant at Delaware U where I found out some things—a lot of things, things most people don't know."

"Why don't you say what you mean?" he snapped. "Why do you always have to beat around the bush?"

Suddenly I realized that I was caught in the middle of a family argument. I also realized that the key to the whole thing, Richard Garrett, was on my side, whereas the other half of it, Hortense Garrett, which I had at first taken for granted, was what was blocking me. Apparently Mr. Garrett didn't know why but meant to find out.

"Hortense, will you please tell us what your objection is? I confess, this thing appeals to me a lot more than hospitals do or some angle on education or the various eleemosynary activities I'm constantly being asked to support—as an outlet for this money that's piling up, and—"

"Richard, it also appeals to me, as I said. I'm for it. I'll be glad to help Dr. Palmer in any way I can. If you want to endow his institute, that's fine, but I won't be its den mother, which is what I think you want."

"Well, somebody has to be."

"Somebody else, not me."

"That was a song."

"I know."

He sat there, snapping his nails against his ballpoint. He was obviously annoyed, but no more annoyed than I was. To come so close and yet miss depressed me. He asked: "Will you give me a memo on it, something I can refer to if the subject ever comes up? No hurry. When you get back to Nebraska will be soon enough."

"Maryland," I corrected. "The senator comes from Nebraska, but I'm at the University of Maryland, where his son is a student. He got into a scrape once over marijuana, which I was able to get him out of. It was the beginning of a beautiful friendship."

"Well, I should hope so."

"Where do you live in Maryland?" she asked me.

"College Park. It's a little town near the District—"

"Oh, I've been to College Park. Are you driving there now?"

"Why—yes, of course."

"He's putting ideas in my head," she said, turning to her husband.

"Oh," he said vaguely, "you mean that car?"

"*That* you left there," she finished for him, sounding a bit waspish. "I was going down with Jasper tonight to bring it back, but—"

"I'm sure Dr. Palmer would be more entertaining company, if he cares to give you a lift." Then, to me: "Would you haul my wife down to Washington when you go?"

"Of course. I'd love to."

For a moment I must have given it a blank stare, because they started talking at the same time, explaining that for various reasons having to do with AR-MALCO, the conglomerate he was president of, he maintained a branch office in Washington and an apartment in Watergate. Three times a week a courier—Jasper—went down there at night with a pouch containing correspondence, memos, and tapes and then drove back in the morning with a pouch from the other end. Mr. Garrett had left the Cadillac at the Watergate apartment some days before when he had business with a friend who had brought him back in his private plane. Mrs. Garrett had expected to drive down with Jasper to bring the car back, but fortunately, here I was instead.

For a mement I glimpsed the world of patents, lawyers, lobbyists, and fixers that they lived in, but then, there she was, wagging her finger at me and bending forward so that those attachments bulged.

"And you stop sulking!" she said. "I really am for your institute. I mean to help you get it, just so long as you leave *me* out. In fact, I have one or two ideas that could actually get you somewhere."

"Go to it, Dr. Palmer," Mr. Garrett said with a kind of grim look. "At least you'll have her for two hours as your captive audience."

"No, *I'll* have him for two hours as *mine*."

Apparently her bag was already packed for the trip she was to take, because it took only a minute for the Swedish maid to bring it, as well as two coats—one a sort of light spring cape and the other a standard mink. Mr. Garrett took the coats and I took the bag after putting on my own coat and hat, and we went downstairs to the parking lot. I put her bag in the trunk of my car and the coats on the back seat. Then I helped her in.

Mr. Garrett put his head in the window and kissed her. Then he came around to my side of the car and shook hands. Nothing more was said about the institute project. He stepped back and waved as I started the motor and drove out to the street.

When we stopped at the first light and I turned the air-conditioner on, I could smell her. It annoyed me that I wanted her. I was still sulking, and not feeling very friendly toward her, but I felt the same hot lech I had felt when she swept into the living room. I tried to fight it off, with no success whatsoever.

"The light's green," she said quietly, and for one throbbing moment I thought she meant *her* light.

"Oh—thanks." My voice sounded as though I were inside a bass drum.

2

Not much was said until we were outside
Wilmington, rolling on Route 40, when she suddenly
sounded off: "Dr. Palmer, to clear up why I'm interested in your institute and at the same time want no
connection with it—no personal connection, that
is. My husband's interest in it is genuine. He respects,
reveres, achievement, which is what biography
honors, so there's nothing phoney about what he told
you. Just the same, there's a little more to it than what
was said, on his side as well as mine. Genuine interest
or not, his immediate concern is to use this thing as
bait, to dangle it in front of me, to get me to take it
over so that we'll shift our base to Washington—our
secondary base, that is—because, of course,
Wilmington would still be home. He thinks
that by giving me this toy, I'll be so excited about
it, so excited about the prospect of running a high-
toned salon for the great, the near-great, and the
would-be-great who'll be getting themselves written
up, that I'll fall all over myself to move down and
become the new Marjorie Merriweather Post, pa-
troness of the arts, encourager of the intelligent-
sia, and chief cook and bottlewasher of all that's

fine and beautiful. I will—in a pig's eye. What's your name?"

"Palmer."

"Your first name, Dr. Palmer?"

"Oh. Lloyd."

"Mine's Hortense, if you'd like to call me that."

"Hortense, I'd be honored."

"Lloyd, the reason is simple, and it's not subject to change after a sales talk, even from you. In Wilmington I'm a great big beautiful frog in the biggest puddle on earth, and I'm not trading that off for something tiny, like a tadpole in a millpond, which is what I'd be in Washington."

"Washington is tiny?"

"Compared with Wilmington, yes."

"I never heard that."

"Now you have."

"Just how do you measure ponds?"

"With money. How do you?"

"Why, with power, for one thing."

"Money *is* power."

"That's one of those spread-eagle statements that's true every foot of the way, not true for every inch. In other words, it's as true as you think it is, but that still leaves the beautiful frog. She is beautiful—every inch, every foot, every yard—"

"Every mile? I'm not that tall."

"Get on with what you started to say. Are you talking about Du Ponts or what?"

"Something wrong with Du Ponts?"

"Not that I know of, no."

"They don't blow their horn, that's true. It's one of the characteristics of money that it does not like its name in the papers—except for pictures, of course.

18

For us beautiful frogs, that's permitted, and I confess that I like it. I like seeing my photograph in print, with my shadows touched up just a bit with mascara. Do you like my shadows?"

"I took them for real."

"They *are* real. But for the camera—"

"O.K., I dote on your shadows. May we get on?"

"Which way is *on*?"

"Is your husband hooked up with the Du Ponts?"

"Lloyd, I don't know, and I'm not at all sure he does either. The whole thing is an interlock so complicated that people have gone mad trying to figure it out. He could be hooked up with them—by stock they hold in his companies, by dummy names on the books, so he wouldn't even know it. Possibly he is, but he doesn't think so, I gather from the little he talks about it, and neither do I. He has reasons for not telling anyone, and I have mine, but mine are simple: the way they act when we go to their houses for dinner and when they come to mine. In general, Du Ponts sell chemistry—processes, dyes they know how to make, fibers they cook out of oil and spin into cloth like nylon, seat covers, stockings. Richard, however, sells *things*. He boasts that he knows a thing from a thing, like tractors and bulldozers and carts, and boats, boats of all sizes and shapes. If you had met him at his office, you'd see the scale models he has there, of everything he makes. But, of course, just like General Motors, all those things need paint, as well as the other things Du Pont has for sale. So he doesn't hurt them; he *helps* them."

"Where does General Motors come in?"

"Well, it's a Du Pont thing."

"Are you sure?"

"Lloyd, on something like that, no one is ever sure. But it has been and, so far as I know, still is . . . mainly."

I was so astonished that I could think of nothing to say for some time.

Suddenly she asked: "How does Wilmington look to you now?"

"Bigger."

"It'll grow on you. Getting back to Richard, there's another reason for Du Pont respect: they're a bit recent compared with him. They came around 1800, pushed out by the French Revolution, and went into the gunpowder business. Then came Napoleon, our War of 1812, and all sorts of things such as our canals which used powder to blow out stumps. One thing led to another, so they got bigger and bigger and bigger. But Richard's ancestors were here long before that. They came over with William Penn and took land on the Delaware. Just to show how filthy rich Richard is, he still has some of that land, and I think Du Ponts respect it."

"Well, I would—"

"Okay, but being cheap doesn't help."

"I beg your pardon?"

"If I were *hauling* a girl somewhere, I'd give her something to eat."

"Oh! Oh! Oh! Yes, of course."

"But not just yet!"

She gave me a playful pat and held up her hand, and there it was—the gorge of the Susquehanna passing under us, one of the world's great sights. She stared, then whispered: "It's so beautiful, I always want to inhale it!"

"Then let's both inhale."

20

Soon we were in Havre de Grace and I pulled in at a roadside joint on the far side of town. We went in and sat at the counter and had hotdogs on rolls, buttermilk, apple pie a la mode, and coffee. She wolfed everything down, then sat sipping her coffee and breathing through her nose. Then we were in the car again.

"Young man in a dinner jacket?" she said. "What kind?"

"Actually, I have two—one black, one red—or, say maroon. I didn't like it at first. The satin lapels were too shiny. But I had them changed to cross-grained silk. Now I like it fine."

"I wonder if I will."

"Just for your info, *I'm* the one wearing it."

"Well, just for *your* info, I'm the one that'll be presenting it, with you inside, at dinner, when I introduce you to money—and, my sweet, I do mean money, millions and millions and millions of it—in an effort to get you your institute. But if your red dinner jacket gets a laugh, we lose before we really go to bat. Why don't we stop at your place so I can have a look?"

"Listen, *I* like the goddam coat."

"Why the pash goddam?"

"I don't want my clothes inspected."

She studied me for a moment and then asked: "What's with the apartment, Lloyd?"

"Nothing—that I know of."

"There has to be, from the shifty way you're acting."

"It's a perfectly good condo. My mother left it to me. Now, if you don't mind, let's talk about something else."

"What's there. A wife you haven't mentioned?"

21

"I'm not married."

"Lloyd, if I find you the money, they'll want to know about you—all kinds of things, like your background and whether you have what it takes to run a biographical institute—or any institute. And why shouldn't they know? After all, how you live is part of it. On top of that, there's *you*. You're not *un*interesting, you know. They wouldn't be human if they didn't want to know you better."

It seems to me now that she said quite a bit more, but I must not have had the right answers, because all of a sudden she said: "Our apartment is in East Watergate. It's at 2500 Virginia Avenue, if you know where that is."

"I do. I know East Watergate."

It was a haughty way of saying forget about College Park and the warthog that had an apartment there. For some time we rode in silence—to Baltimore, through the tunnel, and onto the freeway to Washington. But when I took the turnoff for College Park she said nothing. I came to the Accomac, where I lived, and pulled into the parking lot back of it. I shut the motor off and, still sitting behind the wheel, spoke my piece very stiffly.

"O.K., there *is* something about my apartment. It was my mother's before she died. It was where she lived, with her son a sort of a lodger. As such, it was a beautiful place for a middle-aged woman to call home. But for the son it has caused smiles on faces that did not, *not*, NOT get invited back. So if you do any smiling—"

"What is there to smile at, Lloyd?"

"The decor, I suppose you would call it, consists of Sonny Boy's career. Pictures of him by the dozen, by

22

the score, maybe even by the hundred—doing everything from riding his Shetland pony to getting his Ph.D. Which was fine for Mommy's apartment. But for Sonny Boy to call it *his*, that has a peculiar look. If you want to laugh, go ahead. But it will be the last time you will. I like it, the way I like the dinner jacket. And if you don't—"

"Calm down, Lloyd."

"O.K., let's go up."

We got out of the car and I locked it. I said: "I usually go in the back way, through the basement and up in the freight elevator. But today, in your honor, we can go around front and make a grand entrance through the lobby."

"I think we should use the back way."

I must have looked surprised, because she explained: "We don't know who's in the lobby, who might remember the beautiful frog whose picture they saw in the paper."

"Then through the basement it is."

I unlocked the basement door and led to the freight elevator where I stood with her, feeling foolish while it creaked upward. At the seventh floor we got off and I unlocked the door to apartment 7A. Then I bowed her into my apartment. For a moment she was behind me as I hung up my coat in the guest closet in the vestibule. When I turned, she was under the arch between the vestibule and the living room, her mouth parted, her eyes roving around the room. At last, without looking at me, she said in a reverent whisper: "Lloyd, how could anyone laugh? How could you even imagine that I would? It's beautiful, simply *beautiful!*"

23

If it weren't for the pictures, I'd have been proud of it myself. The room wasn't as big as the drawing room of her place, but it was still pretty big, bigger than most living rooms. On three sides were bookshelves six feet high—solid on the long side where there were no windows and broken on the side with the arch and fireplace. On the fourth side of the room was a large picture window which looked out on the university campus. The view was grassy, fresh, and green.

She moved to the middle of the room where she kept turning around. "It's the books that make me lower my voice. They throw a hush over any room. We have what we call 'the library.' It's full of reference books. Who was Moody?"

"John Moody? Financial writer, I think."

"Yes! *Annual Report of Earnings!* I never go into that room. . . . What are these books? Biographies?"

"A lot of them, yes."

"And you've read them?"

"Well, that's what I buy them for. I think I've read most of them. A lot of them, like *Bancroft's Chronicles of the Builders,* nobody's really read. But I have them. If I want to find out who Kit Carson was, it's in there."

"I'll bite. Who *was* Kit Carson?"

"A scout."

"Never heard of him . . . Oh! There's one I *have* read—*R.E. Lee.*"

"Nice job Freeman did on it."

"I bought it when I was a girl. Paid my girlish money for it. I fell for the beautiful binding. I just love scarlet. And that reminds me to look at your jacket." She started for the door but stopped by the cocktail table to look at an enlarged portrait photograph that

24

was over the fireplace. She asked: "Is that who I think it is?"

"My mother, yes."

"Damned good-looking."

"Beautiful, I'd call her."

"I wouldn't. Beauty, let's face it, is slightly dumb. She wasn't. That face is smart. It can't be fooled."

"With money, it couldn't be."

"The hair, gray, almost white, *is* beautiful. That I admit. The face—those soft, round features, a bit like yours—is beautiful, too. But the eyes see more than beauty cares about. You say she was good with money?"

"Better than my father." I waved at his picture which was on a shelf off by itself. "He was a politician and real estate man. In Prince Georges County they're practically the same thing. He was very proud of my mother—for all the wrong reasons. He died when I was ten years old without finding out how smart she was. What he doted on was her family which came in the *Ark*."

"'Well? Didn't he? Didn't we all?"

"Oh, not *that* Ark. Noah's if that what you mean. The other one, more important here in Maryland. The first settlers came in the *Ark* and the *Dove* and landed in St. Mary's County—the next one down the line. He was always talking about how high-born she was."

"Then you were high-born, too?"

"I don't do much about it. And neither did she."

"Wait till Richard hears about *this*."

"But when my father died, she went to town with what he left her, and doubled it and tripled it and quadrupled it—"

25

"And quintupled it, I'll bet."

"At least. But she wasn't tight with it. She would help anyone out."

"Rich people are often like that. So is you-know-who."

"Just the same, when money saw her come in the door, it would come over for a pat on the head before snuggling into her handbag."

"The more you talk, the more I like her."

"She left me very well off. I don't have to work."

"I'm so glad to hear it."

Her eyes half closed on that, and suddenly I felt foolish. I had forgotten, just for that long, how rich she was. Suddenly she said: "The coat, where is it?"

"My bedroom, I'll show you."

"I'll find it."

She was gone a few minutes. I heard drawers being opened and shut. Then she was back, saying: "The coat's fine and the dark-blue trousers are just right. But those light-blue puff-bosomed shirts are an inspiration. Lloyd, they'll love you. You'll look like just what you are, a high-born Maryland gentleman being gracious to his nouveau riche friends. I'll be proud to present you. I can hardly wait."

"You're putting me on."

"No, I'm not. Do you have a red tie?"

"Yes. Of course I have a red tie."

"Just wanted to know. I forgot to look."

She began making the rounds of the pictures, stopping at one of a little girl beside two oxen yoked to a cart. "Who is she?"

"My mother, when she was little. At that time, in

26

St. Mary's County, they used oxen all the time."

"As I said, the more I know about her, the more I like her."

In front of a picture of me with a pony, she let out a string of yelps. "Oh! Oh! Oh! I always wanted a pony and never had one! What was his name?"

"Brownie."

"And look at his fuzzy forelock."

"He didn't like for it to be pulled. Try it, and he'd bite you, and bite you to mean it."

"I would have patted his nose."

"That he didn't mind."

She pointed at a football mounted on a rack. "What's that about?"

"Touchdown I scored against Navy. They gave me the ball to keep."

"Then you played?"

"That's right. My senior year I was captain."

"But not professionally?"

"It didn't interest me that way. And to be realistic about it, in professional football, at 185, I'd have been a midget."

"Yes, of course; you're really quite tiny."

She went on, moving sideways, while I stood behind her, watching the twitch of her bottom while trying not to. She admired pictures of me taking my bachelor's degree, my master's, and finally, my doctor's, stepping in close to inspect that one and saying: "Just making sure they didn't cheat you on that costume. It's really a gold tassle."

"Yes, they gave me the works."

She moved on to me throwing a pass in some game. Then suddenly she sat down as though collapsed and began staring at me.

"Mrs. Garrett—Hortense! Is something wrong?" She didn't answer me. "Are you ill?" I asked, shaking her.

She still didn't answer. Then a lech that felt like a sea-nettle detached itself from the seat of my pants, moved to my rear, and started crawling up my backbone. I put one arm around her and the other under her knees and lifted. "No, no, no!" she moaned.

I started for the arch, and she kicked and twisted and struggled. One leg slipped clear and fell down. I hung onto the other one and marched on, through the arch, through the foyer and hall to the door of my room. She had closed it. I kicked it open and carried her in. I dumped her on the bed and started peeling her clothes off. I stripped off her coat, the pants of her pantsuit, the panties, bra, stockings, and shoes. When she was naked I picked them up and dropped them on a chair in a pile. She jumped up and darted for them. I grabbed her, held her, and began undressing myself. One-handed, it was a job, but it didn't take long. When I was naked, too, I pulled the spread back. Then I rolled her in and climbed in beside her. At last, when I held her to me, her mouth found mine, and from there on in, it was volcanic.

3

We lay close for a long time in each other's arms, mingling breath. Sometimes she kissed my throat but in an odd way, as though there was something special about it. In between, little by little, my mind came out of the fog. Thoughts began to run through it again. I remembered my sulk, the resentment toward her for blocking me off from her husband and his support of my institute. I wondered what had become of it. All I felt now was reverence, or something like it, for the lift she'd given me, up so high I thought I was in the clouds. I tried to think about it. Then I was inhaling the scent of her hair—so warm, clean, fragrant.

She opened her eyes and whispered: "Why did you do that to me?"

"Do what to you?"

"I would call it rape."

"Then who am I to argue?"

"I did my best to stop you. You can't say I didn't. But no, you had to go on by main force, by brute force. You're very strong, you know."

"Yes, so I've been told."

"Well? I asked you something."

"Why I raped you—?"

"I wish you'd tell me."

"My first answer to why is, why not? Why wouldn't I rape you? The way your bottom twitched there in the living room as you looked at my pictures—first a step to the left, then another step, and for each and every step, a twitch."

"You rape every twitchy bottom?"

"I never saw one before."

"That's not a very good answer."

"You want a better one?"

"I wish you'd give me the real one."

"You wanted me to, that's why."

She wilted and closed her eyes. After a long time, she whispered: "Yes—I wanted you to. I may as well admit it. I fought you off, did everything I knew. And yet I was praying, not that it wouldn't happen, but that it would. Think of that, Lloyd; I actually *prayed*. I tried to get God on the side of that monstrous thing! I've never done that before! With anyone! Except as my vows permitted, except in marriage, I mean! Do you understand what I'm saying? Do you believe me?"

"I knew it without your telling me."

"Lloyd, it's the truth."

"Speaking of God—"

"You believe in Him, don't you?"

"Yes . . . You know who invented what we did?"

"What do you mean, *invented*?"

"*He* did."

"That's a strange idea."

"Well? Who else? Who else could have? The greatest invention in the history of the world. Or maybe you know a better one?"

"Just the same, it was wrong."

30

"Are you sure?"

"It was invented partly to test us."

"How do you know it was?"

"That's the terrible part. It seemed so *right*!"

"Can we get on, Hortense?"

"*On*? To what?"

"The nitty-gritty."

"Which is?"

"I was hit by a truck. What were you hit by?"

". . . a truck."

With that, we stopped talking. We held each other close again, then pulled back and looked at each other. After awhile she whispered: "The biggest truck in the world, so big it frightens me. But because it was big, we must do what it says we must. We have to be true to it, Lloyd. We must know it was a truck, not just a motorbike."

"What are you getting at?"

"It must never happen again."

"I don't get the connection."

"If it was that big, it had to mean something. And if it did, we dare not besmirch it. If it was just desire, then it was cheap and meaningless. But you say you were hit by a truck, and I certainly was. So it was big. So it took us, without any warning. But now we *are* warned. We know what can happen. We're no longer caught by surprise. So, all right, about what happened, life is like that. Perhaps God will forgive us. But it cannot—must not—ever happen again."

I'm trying to remember what she said, but even now it blurs for me. One thing doesn't necessarily lead to another. But at the time, I didn't argue. I just said: "That's how you want it?"

"It's how it has to be."

31

"O.K., then, so be it. Kiss me."

She kissed me in a happy, carefree way, whispering: "That's one thing about you, Lloyd, that I could feel from the moment I laid eyes on you. You're decent."

"Climb on."

"On? Where?"

"My stomach."

"Do you mean what I think you mean?"

"I have impulses."

"But you just promised that it would not happen again."

"I promised that you wouldn't be raped, and you won't be. So climb on. Girl on top can't be raped. All she need do is slide off."

"Dear God, please don't let me."

"Suppose He's pulling for *me*?"

"Lloyd, please don't make me!"

"I'm inviting you, that's all. I can have it engraved, if you like, but it takes a little time and—"

"You're tempting me!"

"Damn it, get on!"

"Oh! . . . Oh! . . . Ohhh!"

It lasted longer that time, but then we were quiet and she lay in my arms again. I said: "Suppose I told you that I loved you? Would you laugh at me?"

"I'd bat you one if you didn't."

"O.K., then, that's settled."

"Swak."

"Could I have that again?"

"S-W-A-K. Sealed With A Kiss. You love me, and that makes me happy."

"O.K., that covers me. How about you?"

32

"Lloyd, don't make me say it."

"Why me and not you?"

"I'm married. That's why not me."

"Let's go into that."

"Please. I don't want to."

"We have to."

"Then all right, let's. But there's nothing to say. I'm married. If I was so stupid, so utterly without sense, as to forget it for that long and then forget it once again—I'm still married. That's the beginning of it, and the end. There's nothing more to say."

"How tight?"

"What do you mean, 'how tight'?"

"Does he do it to you or not?"

She moaned and broke into sobs. I popped her bottom and said: "Yes or no?"

At last she moaned: "No!"

"Now we're getting somewhere. But it calls for explaining—kind of. Why doesn't he? Did you have a fight? Is there another woman? Or what?"

"We didn't have any fight and there's no other woman that I know of. We weren't in love at all. It didn't figure in our prenuptial companionship, if that's what it's called. We met at a party my uncle gave—his big annual stinkaroo, his pay-back bash for the dinners he'd been invited to during the year. He was my father's brother, and we weren't rich, but he was. And my mother, who's a Chapman from Chester, studied nursing when she was young and married just after getting her cap. But she looked after Uncle Allen, especially at his parties, so his blood pressure wouldn't shoot up. But this time she came down with a case of shingles, and I had to take charge. I remembered names, got them all right—also steered things,

33

especially the caterer's end, which wasn't done very well. Richard was there, admiring me—my computer mind, he called it, which he ascribed to social training I really didn't have. I was brought up well enough, but keeping the names straight—which was what impressed him so—had nothing to do with it. My last year at Delaware, I was a teaching assistant—you know, the Simonette Legree who marks examination papers—and a favorite indoor sport she has to watch out for is where one student takes the course and another, the examination. So she acquires a considerable skill at telling which name goes with which face. As for the steering, which also impressed Richard, I ran the Rodney Dining Hall one year—and there, believe me, you'd *better* learn how to steer."

"Where did the names and steering come in?"

"I told you—as social graces. Richard began to picture me as his hostess, up under the sky at his apartment in Wilmington."

"Now I get it. Go on."

"So I was excited. Who wouldn't be? After all, he was Richard Garrett. He got a hostess and I got a big financier. But he didn't get any wife and I didn't get any husband. A marriage is made in bed, which, I think, can be heaven if two people love each other; but ours was a flop. I don't know what the trouble was. He tried and I tried, and we both tried and tried and tried—telling ourselves that when we got used to each other, it would be all right. But it never was all right. We never were suited for marriage. All the trying in the world wouldn't have been any help. I began having dreams, horrible dreams I'd rather not talk about. Then when I had a miscarriage, it all came to a head, and I knew I couldn't go on. When I got home from the hospital, though, I found that he felt the same way. So we slept in separate rooms. It helped that while I was gone, our Swedish housekeeper, who had lived in, had gotten some kind of cable from Stockholm and had to go home. So no embarrassment was involved. I made the beds, and when Karen came in the morning, there was nothing for her to notice. At last we were happy. I loved entertaining his friends; and believe me, I do it well. He's nice, perfectly wonderful, to *my* friends, except that he has this notion that we ought to move to Washington. What he really means is that *I* ought to move to Washington. Now, does that explain it better? Why I can't get mixed up with your institute?"

"Yes, at last it makes sense." But then I remembered. "Except for one thing," I said. "Why did you do it at all? We agree, I think, that I am overwhelmingly irresistible and all that. But you were underwhelmed plenty until you came to that picture of me heaving a pass in a football game. Where did that come in? What did it have to do with football?"

"It's a long story."

"We have all day . . . all night."

After awhile she said: "It was seeing your neck, your bare neck, your beautiful bare neck, in that picture . . . that left me . . ."

"Yes? Where?"

"Shook to the heels."

"Give. Say it." ———

"When I was in high school, I was invited for a visit to the home of a girl who lived in Maryland on a farm in the Greenspring Valley where her father raised racehorses. And one morning we hid out in the carriage house next to the stables, to see a stallion serve a

35

mare. It was terribly exciting, more so than I'd have believed. He courted her like a schoolboy, prancing around in front of her, before finally going through with what he was there to do. Once, for a second or two, he was only a few feet from us—where we were peeping through the window—and for that long he arched his neck. We could have reached out and touched it. We could actually see the beat of his heart in the pulse of one of the blood vessels. Lloyd, it actually throbbed. Well, one day in Newark, when Delaware was playing Maryland, this Maryland boy threw a pass, and I could see his neck, which was bare. And it throbbed the way that stallion's had. Lloyd, when I saw that picture just now, with the same bare neck showing, when I knew I was in the same room with that boy, with that neck, that beautiful neck, I had to sit down. But how did you know? How *could* you know how I felt?"

I told her about the sea nettle. "Strange," she whispered. "You knew just by looking at me?"

"Let's say I hoped. Don't forget, I wanted you bad, from the moment I laid eyes on you."

"They told me that your name was Palmer—Brisket Palmer. I memorized it."

"Yes, and how that came about was: My football jersey itched. It was wool, and it felt like fleas. So I found a cotton shirt to wear underneath it, and that did it except for the neck. So my mother snipped it out with some buttonhole scissors. That left my neck bare. Every sportswriter decided the idea was to show off a thing of beauty. So one of them called me 'the Brisket'—and it stuck. Just the media being fair and impartial and scrupulous, as usual."

"It was a thing of beauty, and still is. So firm, so

36

round."

"Sign of physical strength, which I have."

"Did you know it has a mole, a tiny double mole, beside the Adam's apple? It looks like a little hourglass."

"I shave over it every morning."

She kissed it, then went on: "Now I'll really be depraved. You know what? If such a thing were possible, if it could happen again, I'd climb on board once more and—".

"Well, what's impossible about it?"

"You mean it can be done? Three times in one afternoon?"

"To a studhorse, with something as good-looking as you, all things are possible. Up, pretty creature, and on!"

"Lloyd, I love you, I love you, I love you."

It was the last carefree moment we had for some time.

4

She rolled off, snuggled close, and lay for a long time without speaking. Then: "Lloyd, I've been thinking. I could give a little dinner and ask about six couples and let you do your stuff—talk about biography while your great big chest bulged your puff-bosom shirt—and hope one of the six would take the bait. But a better idea, I think, would be a little dinner for six. You, some dame I'll think of to round it out nicely, Richard, me, and a couple I know of named Granger who're not Du Ponts but are filthy rich and are already literary to some extent. They were friends of that pair of Du Ponts who were friends of the Henry Menckens—so they'll know what you're talking about. I imagine they might get a kick out of being a part, the main part, of something intellectually important. And I don't see how Richard could make any trouble. He'd look awfully small, trying to."

"But why would he?"

"I told you why."

I thought that over and asked: "You think he's out? Unless you change your mind?"

"I won't change my mind."

"I know, but is he out, once and for all?"

"Why do you ask?"

"Oh, I don't know. Just Brisket Palmer who hates to give up. He's my one bird-in-hand, you know. Before going for birds-in-the-bush, I thought we might figure an angle on him."

I probably said more, because I suddenly realized that I was talking along without getting any reaction. When I looked at her again, she was up on one elbow, staring hard at me. "Lloyd, you wouldn't take advantage, would you?"

"How 'take advantage'?"

"Of me. With Richard."

Now, so help me, the only advantage I had on my mind, at least until then, was how to get in sync with her twitch. It hadn't occurred to me, as apparently it hadn't to her until just then, that if I wanted to take advantage of the situation, I now had her over a barrel. For several moments we had it, eyeball to eyeball. We both knew what she meant. But I couldn't quite own up, and my mouth took over, to fudge. "How— make it plainer, please. How could I take advantage?"

"By betraying me, Lloyd."

"I ask you to make it plainer, and you—"

"By telling Richard about it, what went on in this bed today—which would solve all of his problems, dirt cheap, as he would regard it—as well as all your problems. He'd be rid of me without having to pay me a cent, and you'd have your institute, sealed, delivered, and paid for. Because, of course, the amount you say it would cost—twenty million, I think it was—would be nothing to him, compared with what he would owe me as a property settlement in a regular divorce. Cheating wives don't get paid, as I think you very well know. So that's how you could take advantage. And for this institute, if you can, you will."

"Just like that—chitty-chitty, bang-bang?"

"I think so. Yes."

"Couple of things wrong with that theory, though."

"What things?"

"His reaction, for one thing. The way he *might* act, correct it. But, of course, as we lie here, we can't be sure *what* he would do. Most likely, if I went to him with this tale, he would kick me out but quick. Then he'd go to you, and you'd tell him . . . what?"

"Why, the truth, I think."

"Are you sure?"

"Of course I'm sure! Why—" She must have talked for ten minutes, saying how sure she was. Finally I cut in: "Or in other words, you'd lie, figuring it was my word against yours. Then he decides to take your word, and I'm out and you're in. Chitty-chitty, bang-bang."

She closed her eyes and lay there a long time. "But he could take *your* word, Lloyd."

"Okay, I'm out and you're out. So—"

"So *what*?"

"We're out together—out there, in here."

"You mean you think that after you had cost me my marriage, I'd come sneaking back to you? How stupid can you get?" She paused. "I see myself doing it, Lloyd."

"I see myself doing it, too—in a pig's eye, I do. The whole idea is silly, so silly as to be completely ridiculous. Why, the idea of my going to him—"

"You wouldn't have to go."

"You mean I could beam it to him by radio?"

"You could telephone and not say who you were."

"And he wouldn't recognize my voice? Or have any

41

idea who it was that would know what you did in this bed? How stupid can *you* get? You, I'm talking about."

"You could send an anonymous card."

"Which, with the money he has, he could have traced in two days. Come on, make sense."

"Would you take advantage of me or not?"

"I told you, make sense."

"I want an answer—yes or no?"

"Okay, then, no."

After a long pause she said: "I don't believe you."

"Why not?"

"Because you're not looking at me."

"I'm looking at you now—straight. Now, what do my eyes say?"

"Lloyd, they say you're lying."

"I wouldn't know how to make them look any straighter."

"They look too straight."

"I don't know any other way to look."

"That's it, Lloyd. You *would* take advantage of me."

To change the subject, I pulled the covers down, turned her on her stomach, and massaged her backside a little, with good hefty slaps, one-two-three, so that it sounded like artillery. Pretty soon I asked: "Hey? Why don't you beat me back?"

"I don't feel that way about it."

"What way is that?"

"I don't feel friendly."

"O.K., I do, but if you don't, that's how we play it, anything to please a lady. So, call."

"What?"

"Get on that phone, there on the night table, and

call—your husband, to say you've changed your mind. If I get credit for being a rat, I may as well get the advantage."

"You'd take it—it's what I said."

"*I* said call, so call."

"No use calling now. He was due in Philadelphia late this afternoon and won't be back till tonight."

"Then call him tonight."

"All right."

Suddenly she started crying. I took her in my arms and whispered that I loved her. "Get on," I said.

"Oh no! That's over!"

"Once more, to prove that I love you—and that you love me."

"I couldn't love a rat."

"Rat loves you, though."

"Dear God, don't let me!"

"Hortense, didn't you hear me?"

Turned out that she did.

At last, early that evening, we got up. Still undressed, she made the bed while I sat and watched. She admired the bed. When I said my mother had had it made to be slightly smaller than the beds in the stores, she looked it over again, touching it with her fingers. "It's so simple," she said. "Just the four turned posts and a turned piece in between, at the head, with the two side boards cut down in the middle. That's all. And it's maple; it's not Wallace Nutting. I'm getting a bit tired of him."

"Keep on. I love those friendly words."

"Toward *her*! Your *mother*!"

"Almost forgot yourself, didn't you?"

"I don't forget anything."

Then we bathed, she in the tub and I in the glassed-in shower. When we toweled off facing each other, her attachments shook breathtakingly. She said: "Heaven only knows what happens now. It's my infertile time of the month—*supposed to be!* Heaven only knows how it's *going* to be."

After we dressed, we went down in the freight elevator and out the back way to the car. I took her to the Royal Arms where the specialty is roast beef, and we gobbled down the whole thick portion. But even while we were eating, she kept questioning me about biography and biographers. "Especially where I come in, or can come in, if you still insist on that call." Her questions were penetrating, so much so that they surprised me, and I sharpened up on my answers, putting things on the line, while she took notes, writing on the back of the menu. She had her mind on it, and insisted: "If I'm to put on this show for Richard, I have to have things straight, so I make sense, so he believes I've changed my mind for the reasons I say I have. I still say it would be much, much better if you didn't make me, Lloyd, if we simply forgot about it."

"I'm not making you, Hortense."

"Oh yes but you are."

"You're going to call so you can sleep."

"I'm going to *what?*"

"It's not me who has this thing on the brain. It's you. You're in my power—that we both know and I know I would never take the advantage I have. But you don't know it, you can't be sure. It's for that reason—pure, yellow-bellied terror—that you're going to put in that call. To be safe from me, as you think."

"If I withdraw my opposition, I will be."

"O.K., whatever you say."

44

"Well? Won't I be? . . . *I better be!*"

"You are now. As you know, but can't be quite sure."

"We go round and round and round."

Watergate's on Virginia, but at her suggestion I parked on New Hampshire around the corner from it. I got out her bag while she got the light coat. She was wearing the mink. We walked around to the marquee, and the doorman came running to take the bag. When he'd disappeared through the door, she turned to me. "Lloyd, you still want me to do it, go through with this?"

"Hortense, it's *you* who wants to do it!"

"Then, okay, I will."

"You want a bump on the backside?"

"I'll stop by your place in the morning, at ten sharp. Please be out front, so I don't have to get out or go in that lobby."

"I'll be there waiting."

"I'll call Richard when I get upstairs. On the way to Wilmington tomorrow, I can tell you what he said."

"Then we'll be together on it."

"Good night."

And she dived through the door without looking back.

5

I spent a bad night, though the beginning of it was nice as I lay there in the dark thinking how well the day had turned out. I even snickered now and then at the way her conscience was working, how, in order to neutralize danger, she was doing the one thing she knew and then blaming it on me. For awhile that seemed pretty funny. Then, down in my gut, something started to twist. I suddenly asked myself if that was how things were, if that was how they really were, if there wasn't perhaps a little more to it. At long last the question popped out in the open: Where did I come in? *How* did I come in? At first, it had seemed to be her doing, the idea of telling Richard that she had switched. But now I made myself face the truth that there was more to it than that, that maybe my eyes were telling her things I hadn't guessed yet even about myself. In other words, deep down inside, I began to suspect that I would take advantage of her, that I would somehow think of a way; that being the case, the way she was acting made sense. But often, when you realize something, you realize it all at once, so that it hits you in the face and things aren't the same anymore. All of a sudden it wasn't quite so funny, what she was about to do. Then out of the dark a hot flash shot at me. It said we were playing with fire, that however the thing turned out, it couldn't turn out well. After a couple of these, I lay there asking myself: Should I go to Wilmington with her? Get out from under, the flashes said, get out while the getting is good, or it's going to explode in your face in a way you'll never forget. I'm human, and all this shook me. Then I thought: nothing risked, nothing gained. In a poker game there comes a time when you shove in your stack or quit with what you've got. And this was like poker, wasn't it?

Then I slept. I knew what I was going to do.

In the morning I spent ten minutes finding keys to give her—to the back door and to the apartment—and putting the keys on a ring. Then I went downstairs and stood under the marquee, feeling like a fool, sure that she wouldn't come.

A bright-green Cadillac turned the corner and came to a stop beside me, and then she was leaning over, unlocking the door so I could get in. She played it straight, saying "Good morning" and commenting on a "beautiful day." I played it the same way, making a point of the car and how nice-looking it was. She said: "It's just a car my husband runs around in." And that seemed to exhaust the subject.

We had gone through the tunnel under Baltimore Harbor before she brought up the call, and when she did, she made it quick: "I simply couldn't say that I had changed my mind. It would have sounded so phoney. I said that you had hinted that you had some idea—an inspiration, you called it, that you would tell him and, of course, me—which would make me change my mind, or at least, so you thought. Then I spent half the night trying to think what your idea

48

was—or is. Whatever. Anyway, I called him at home just now to say that curiosity was killing the cat, that I would bring you back with me to let us hear it in person. Now all you have to do is think up an idea. But if you can't, it's all right with me. You can just get out, thumb a ride back, and forget the whole thing."

"Afraid I couldn't do that."

"I did, it so happens, come up with something myself."

"I'm holding my breath."

"You could name this thing after me."

"Well, of course; I love that idea."

"Then I could realize it would make me a *pretty* big frog in a puddle not too small—and that would be that."

"I would say that's it; we've got it."

"Stop we-ing me."

"I wouldn't mind, at that."

She stomped on the brake, brought the car to a sudden stop in the breakdown lane, and hauled off and gave me a slap that stung for ten minutes. Then she started again. "That may be it," she said. "The question is not what it is, but whether he believes it."

We drove on, two people miles apart. At the river she stared straight ahead, paying it no attention. When we crossed the Delaware line she pulled over and stopped. "Now," she began in a stilted, self-conscious voice; "we're within twenty minutes of Wilmington, and I've stopped here to plead with you to give up this idea of yours, if you still have it, that I recommend to my husband that he accept your proposal that he endow some institute with you in charge. Dr. Palmer, I assure you that if you force me to do this, it can only lead to disaster. What do you say?"

"Give me a minute to think."

"Take as long as you want."

So I thought, or I suppose I did, but as I remember, nothing much went through my head. At last I said: "The idea's not mine; it's yours."

"You're wrong. The idea is yours."

"Have it your way. I won't argue. But it's you, don't forget, who's afraid. And it's you who's trying to cap that fear, stuff it back in the pipe by neutralizing me. Whatever I say to you now, whatever I promise to do, will leave you still afraid, except for this one thing you thought of first, that I be bought off with the institute. I want him to start. Well, so be it. Drive on."

"Rat is flattery."

"Self-deception is worse."

She was to take me to his office, so we drove to a building in downtown Wilmington, which had AR-MALCO chiselled over the entrance. She had barely stopped when a doorman in a maroon uniform was opening the door for her. He bowed and smiled and called her by name. I got out, but by the time I'd walked around, he had handed her down and was saying "Yes'm" when she told him to lock up because her coats and bag were inside. I followed her into the lobby, into a big elevator, then into a reception room where the girl at the desk jumped up and said a bit breathlessly: "Mrs. Garrett, Mr. Garrett's expecting you"—and with a glance at a card—"and Dr. Palmer."

Hortense answered her pleasantly. Then a secretary

50

came out and spoke to her and ushered us into an office. It was an office such as I had never seen—large, with a handsome desk at one end and a fireplace at the other, cocktail table, an oriental rug, copper ashtrays, and gigantic, leather-upholstered sofas in between. But the main items in the room weren't in it, strictly speaking; they were *around* it, on the walls. They were covered with shelves, of redwood, apparently with indirect lighting to illuminate scores of exhibits, scale models of the products ARMALCO made. There were motorbikes, trucks, tractors, trailers, mowers, radios, TVs—and boats. Boats and more boats. Most of the boats—the cruisers, sloops and skiffs—were no more than twelve inches long; but three of them, of regular ships, were six feet long and possibly more, exact to the smallest fitting. I went around peering at them, gasping in astonishment, while Hortense, stretched out on a sofa, listened.

Presently she explained: "My husband has a passion for *things*, as he calls them. The Nutting stuff in the apartment is just the beginning. He says this is what's made him rich. He imagines himself a psychic."

"Some of my best friends are."

"Do you know what *psychic* means?"

"So? What?"

"It means you know the truth without knowing how you know it. There's still time, before he comes in, to pull back from this Rubicon."

"Can't let Caesar skunk me."

I struck a pose, my fingers in my lapel. She winced. "Oh for God's sake, Lloyd, that's Napoleon, not Caesar!"

"Can't let Boney skunk me either."

I didn't notice at first that she had used my given

51

name, the first time all morning. Under my coat my fingers suddenly touched the keys I'd put on the ring for her, which I'd dropped into my shirt pocket. I took them out and offered them to her.

"What's that?"

"Keys. One to the back door of the building, one to my apartment. So the next time you come—"

"The *next* time I *come*! As funny as you are, you should be on television. Do you seriously think there will be a next time for me after the way you've—"

"We *said* we were hit by a truck, and the truck I was hit by has no reverse gear. All I know is, God willing, I'll hope for a next time. And perhaps—"

I reached over and dropped the keys down the front of her blouse, into the V below her neck. Her hand slapped to stop them from slipping down, but in spite of her slapping and grabbing, they slipped down anyway. Suddenly she stopped trying to fumble them out, and lay there staring at me.

"Lloyd," she whispered, "when you said what you did just now, about the truck with no reverse, your eyes didn't lie to me."

"I hope to tell you, they didn't."

"It gives me an idea!"

"Well, Hortense, please—not here!"

"Why not?"

"Because, if it's the idea *I* have—"

"My sweet, there can be only one idea—one real idea." She smiled. "It all depends on the way it's put into effect." Her eyes narrowed until they were slits, glittering as though hornets were crawling on them.

6

What those hornets meant I found out soon enough. Mr. Garrett came in a few minutes later, wearing slacks and lounge coat this time. He nodded amiably to me and bowed in a courtly manner to Hortense.

"Hello," she crooned in a low voice, waving him closer. He went over to her and sat down as she moved to give him room, responding when she pulled him down for a kiss. ". . . and hello," he growled, obviously shaken.

Suddenly I knew what it felt like to suffer.

"Be with you in a minute," he flung over his shoulder to me, bending over her again. I walked to the window and stared out at Wilmington—which isn't much to look at when viewed under such circumstances.

"*Now*," he said. When I turned, he was sitting beside her, holding her hand and patting it. "My wife," he went on, "says you have an idea, something you think will change her mind. I'm listening."

"Well," I said, trying to regain my wits, "I had no idea before—when I was here yesterday, I mean—*why* she felt as she did—"

"Feel as I *do*," she corrected me.

"But she let something drop as we were driving to Washington which put me on the track of a way to work things out so that she can have what she wants—except better—and more of it—"

"I'm curious."

"Mr. Garrett, it seems she's a frog—"

"But a great big beautiful frog—"

"Yes sir, in the biggest puddle on earth."

"My boy, Wilmington's big, I promise you—bigger than I am by far. In some other place, I'd be quite a guy. Here I'm just a piker."

"Dr. Palmer, he's not telling the truth."

"I know that, Mrs. Garrett."

"Richard, when he and I are alone, he calls me Hortense. He's a cheeky son of a bitch."

"I like cheeky guys. They can sell."

He motioned for me to go on. It didn't help matters that she snuggled to him, responding to his pats. But I gritted my teeth and said as if by rote. "However, big as Wilmington is, it's not as big as the earth, and that's the side of the puddle I'm offering her—you and her, but mainly her."

"The earth? What do you mean?"

"Biography is international. The subjects aren't all American, not by any means. One man writes about Caesar, another chooses Napoleon, another Wellesley, the Duke of Wellington. Yesterday, when I spoke of the American preeminence in the field, I may have given the impression that it was a national thing. It isn't. It's international, just as the writers of it are. In other words, if Mrs. Garrett were to take charge of this thing, she would be not a more beautiful frog—as that, of course, is impossible—but a much bigger frog, provided, that is, that you take one obvious step. Pro-

54

vided that you name it for her."

"But I intended to!"

He looked down at her and asked: "Dear? Does Dr. Palmer's idea appeal to you?"

"*Your* idea, if it *was* your idea, does."

"Well, I did intend to, Hortense."

"Then I'm shook to my heels, Richard. Yes, it does appeal to me, that you lay this wreath at my feet." She waited for a moment, while he waited, too, sensing that more was coming. "Richard, I'll be in *Who's Who*."

"You *are* in *Who's Who*."

"Yes, but in my own right, not just as your wife."

"You'll be in Who's Who in the World," I said.

"I never heard of Who's Who in the World."

"You have now."

She still hadn't quite said yes but seemed about to, when she shied away all of a sudden, I suspected to torture me. Anyway, she did. "Oh, I don't know," she burst out. "Isn't it going to look funny? I mean, queer the thing from the outset, to have a woman in charge? After all—"

"Why is it?" I asked in a hot, argumentative way. "Women are great in this field. Look at Fawn Brodie and her sensational biography of Jefferson. Look at Anita Leslie and the fresh stuff she dug up on the Edwardians. And Barbara Tuchman and her book on China, which is primarily a biography of Stillwell."

"What was that name?" Mr. Garrett asked.

"Tuchman, Barbara Tuchman."

"Hold everything."

He got up and went out, leaving us alone for a few minutes.

"Lloyd," she said cordially, "I can't thank you

enough for that idea you gave me. It's going to work out fine—though, of course, not with you. That's the part you forgot. It's the kind of idea that's not restricted at all in how it's put into effect. So I'll have that. I'll be a still larger frog. I'll swim in the puddle you found me—and then I'll kick you out."

"Are you sure?"

"What do you mean?"

"Bitch, I still have you over a barrel."

"That's what you think, Buster."

"I knew I'd heard that name," Mr. Garrett said as he came back in and sat down with a copy of *Who's Who in America* in his lap. "Barbara Tuchman. Did you know, dear, that she was Maurice Wertheim's daughter?"

"Who is Maurice Wertheim?"

"Banker, big shot. The main angel of the old New York Theatre Guild. But I knew him—not well, as a boy knows a man, but *that* well. He was a friend of my father's, and I had enormous respect for him. Friendly, considerate, a little pompous, a bit overfond of the I-cap, but basically decent. And to think that his daughter—"

"She's very eminent," I put in.

"I can see she is. It's in here."

All of a sudden, we agreed that a woman in charge would help, rather than hinder, and he asked: "Well, dear? Is it settled?"

"Richard," she said in a stage whisper, "do you know what we could do if Dr. Palmer weren't here?"

"I guess that means me," I gulped.

"I guess it does," he said without looking up. "I'm due in London next week, but you'll be hearing from me as soon as I get back."

56

The horrible, jealous twinge that shot through me told me that if torture was her idea, it was working, and well. I was still atremble when I reached the street, walking along in the sunlight, wondering where I was. It was several minutes before I had it: I was on my way to the bus stop to ride back to Baltimore and then change for College Park. But I still wasn't quite through. I was stumping along when I heard running footsteps behind me, and I realized that someone was calling me. I turned, and there was the secretary, Miss Immelman, she now said her name was. "I called as you went out the door," she said breathlessly, "but when I went out in the hall, you were gone. I was to give you the apartment number, so you can call there in case. Mr. Garrett told me to when he came out to get that book."

She handed me a card with a phone number written on it in a woman's hand, area code 302. "He wasn't sure you had it," she said, still out of breath.

"Thanks ever so much. I didn't."

"The senator has, but—"

"I'm not the senator, am I?"

7

The next three days were bad, worse than I had thought they could be. I had what I wanted. I had used her to put it across, and I *had* put it across. That being the case, it didn't seem inevitable that I would suffer much, after only one day with her, from the fact that he was back in her bed. I went through hell. I'd think of her eyes, her attachments and how they shook, the way her bottom twitched. A hundred times I owned up to the fact that it wasn't an afternoon's fun I could forget and go on with my life. It was as big as I'd told her it was. The worst of it was that even on fundamentals, I wasn't sure it would stick, because there was that remark she'd made, that after becoming a frog in a larger puddle, she would throw me out. I kept telling myself that on that point, at least, I was safe, that she couldn't throw me out without risking my revenge, which I could take any time simply by calling Mr. Garrett at the number Miss Immelman had given me and telling him. I thought, *at least that stops her from talking*; but then: *if he charged her with what I said, she could simply say that I raped her, that she had meant to spare him the truth; but since I was playing dirty, the truth was all she had left.* When I got that far with the thought, I can tell you, it hurt.

On the third night I turned to misery's companion, a deck of playing cards, and dealt them out on the cocktail table for a game of solitaire. I had been at it for some time when I heard the freight elevator. I wondered who would be using it at that hour of the night. The elevator stopped at the seventh floor. Then I heard footsteps on the other side of my door. A key clicked in the lock. My heart almost stopped beating. The only people who had ever had keys were my mother before she died, Eliza, the cleaning woman, and Hortense. For some reason, it was my mother I thought of now as the door began to open slowly.

It was Hortense. She closed the door and stood in the foyer, looking at me.

"Well?" she said. "You gave me the keys, didn't you?"

I went clumping over to her, gathered her in my arms, and kissed her—just once. Then I stood back and said: "O.K., I'm glad. I can't pretend I'm not. Now suppose you get the hell out."

"Suppose I *what*?"

"You heard me. Get out."

"Any particular reason?"

"You know why: you don't shack up for two days with him and then start up with me again. Out. Beat it."

"Just like that?"

"Just like that."

"And suppose I don't want to?"

"Then I'll throw you out."

"I don't believe it. Want to bet?"

"Okay," I said, grabbing her, "you're going—*now!*"

"And taking the institute with me?"

I was so angry that I had forgotten about the institute. Suddenly a lump came in my throat and my heart skipped a beat. She came close, her lips skinned back from her teeth.

"Dr. Palmer!" she exclaimed as though greatly concerned. "Are you all right? Oh my! You turned the color of chalk. Should I call a physician? Or administer mouth-to-mouth resuscitation? What do you wish me to do?"

"All right, then, stay."

"Stay? If I—"

"Please."

"That's better. And could we sit down?"

She led the way into the living room where she pushed me into a chair with more strength than I would have thought she had.

"Now!" she went on brightly and cheerily, "*if* I may have your attention, I wish to gloat." She walked away from me, twitching it, then walked back, twitching everything. "Do you like it? Does it give you ideas? Does it remind you of night before last when you were in bed here, alone, at least as we hope, and I was— But need we go into details? Were you imagining my situation, after the coup you arranged, of a bigger pond to swim in and a place in *Who's Who in the World*? I hope it caused you no pain imagining how pitiful I looked there in my bed, waiting, whispering things through the door—"

"Goddam it, shut up."

"No profanity, please. It upsets me."

"Will you, for Christ's sake, knock it off?"

"Beautiful gloat, I love you."

By then it was affecting me as though I had a

cramp, and I was all doubled up in the chair. But all of a sudden she folded, collapsing face down on one of the sofas. I let her lie there awhile. Then I went over to see if something was wrong. I couldn't see that anything was but leaned down when she started to mumble, low and jerky, one or two words at a time. "I thought," she said, or at least I thought she said, "—it was going to be fun—that I would love it, having my gloat. But it wasn't fun at all." And then, after some time: "A gloat's not a gloat; it's not any gloat at all if it's not a gloat." That made no sense, but then suddenly she cleared it up. Turning over, she burst out: "It has to be *real*! It has to be real, and it's not. *He didn't come to me.* He just kissed me and said good night! He was wonderful except for that—had flowers sent over, three beautiful orchids, took me to dinner, said all kinds of lovely things. But he didn't do what I hoped for—and I don't have any gloat! Any *real* gloat, at you! I enjoyed torturing you. I guess I did, if I did, torture you, I mean. You had it coming. You certainly did. But—"

"Shut up."

"Okay, now you know."

"Where is he now?"

" 'Up above the world so high, like a tea tray in the sky.' What's that from?"

"Alice in Wonderland."

"Yes, he's flying to London, but what's there? What's with London to make it a wonderland?"

"You know what I've got a good mind to do? Fan your backside till it has blisters on it and looks like two fried egg yolks."

"O.K., here it is."

She turned over again, pulled up her skirt, and slid

down her pantyhose to give me a full, fair view, and right there on the living room sofa, with half her clothes still on, we resumed our love affair, complete with biting, whispering, and spanking. Afterward, we lay there, holding close. At last she said: "I was close to God. What were you close to?"

"God."

"I'm hungry."

I kissed her, pulled on my clothes, and went out to the kitchen to fix a snack. I had just got out eggs, mushrooms, bacon, juice, bread, and coffee when she joined me, wearing a pair of my pajamas with the legs and sleeves turned up and her own shoes with no stockings inside.

"I found this outfit in your bureau drawer," she said. "Okay to wear it?"

"But of course. Be my guest."

"What are you giving me?"

"Tomato juice, an omelette, bacon, toast, coffee. This hour of the night, I thought you'd rather have Sanka. I might add that you're looking at the champion three-egg-and-mushroom-filler-omelette-maker of Prince Georges County, Maryland. I have special, peculiar skills that—"

"I don't want an omelette."

"Tell me what you do want, please."

"I want two eggs sunny-side up, to look as my backside would have if it had gotten what it deserved—so I know, in lieu of a mirror."

"Sunny-side up, they shall be."

She gulped down her tomato juice, then I made her the eggs. She ate them neat, saying "You're supposed to break the yokes, but I love to put them in whole and squash them with my tongue. These are *nice*."

63

Butter dribbled from the toast onto her chin, and she held it over for me. I said: "Come on, hurry up; that puts ideas in my head."

"They the only ideas you have?"

"If you know a better one—?"

"I don't, but not yet, please. Let's have a polite conversation until my eggs start to digest and ideas come to *my* head."

"Okay, lead the discussion."

But for that, we went in the living room. She stretched out on the sofa, yawned, and said: "I feel like a cat that just lapped up the cream."

"Conversation, please."

"Lloyd, why don't we get acquainted?"

"Well? Aren't we?"

"In a way, yes—in one way, definitely. In other ways, we don't know each other at all. So all right, I'll start it off. As I told you, I was born in Chester, of a shipbuilding family, comfortably well off. Public school, then finishing school for three days, high school, Delaware U., then Richard and marriage at nineteen. Then, hostess, hostess, hostess to Richard's many friends, most of them important, meaning most of them rich. Received and accepted, partly because of my skill as a hostess and partly because of Richard's money. In school, the boys made passes at me. In college they did, too, and I'm not sure I wasn't willing. But the passes were pretty clumsy and nothing came from them . . . The passes weren't clumsy; they were fainthearted. *That's* why I didn't give in. *Your* pass wasn't fainthearted. It was what I called it—rape."

"It was what you wanted, though."

64

"You're damned right, it was what I wanted."

"Shipbuilding family, you say. How many?"

"Ships? Oh, dozens and dozens."

"What size family was it?"

"Oh, well, father, mother—my father died. My mother became a registered nurse, and still looks like one."

"Brothers? Sisters?"

"One brother who died. Now, how about you?"

"About me, not much to tell. Just a guy who was born in Prince Georges County."

"Your father—when did he die?"

"When I was ten."

"And who was *she?* Your mother, I mean."

"Just a St. Marys County girl. Father a bank cashier in St. Marys City. It was on her mother's side—my grandmother's side, that is—that she traced her line back to the *Ark.* I told you about that, I think."

"Which made her aristocracy?"

"I suppose so."

"And you're aristocracy, too?"

"But I don't do much about it."

"Did she?"

"No, but it still meant something to her."

Hortense stared at the picture, then went on. "O.K., so you grew up here where we are, in College Park, is that it?"

"Marlboro, the county seat."

"Oh. Then you moved—?"

"To College Park, here to this apartment, when I entered college—the university, actually. Then football, post-graduate study, and a Ph.D. for me, and all kinds of investments for her. She wasn't grasping or avaricious, at least as far as I know; but money just

65

gravitated to her, all the time. She made more than my father ever saw, and he didn't do too badly. She left me comfortable, even without a job. When she died, it was the worst blow of my life."

"When was this?"

"Little over a year ago."

"Were you in love with her?"

"What do you mean, *in love* with her?"

"I mean, did you like to kiss her?"

"Well, she was my mother, wasn't she?"

"Was it her idea to rip the neck of your jersey?"

"What are you getting at?"

She didn't answer at once, but stared for several moments. Then she asked: "How many girls have you had?"

"Why—one or two, of course."

"You were successful with them?"

"Listen, if they want to, they want to, and that being the case, they do. Use your own judgment."

"How many?"

"No normal guy ever had one before this one now. She's always the first and only."

"That's a very sweet thing to hear you say. How many?"

"Three."

"And they were? Who was the first one?"

"Little waitress in Ocean City my summer as a life-guard."

"Where did you do it with her?"

"On the sand dune up the beach."

"And the second?"

"A student during my sophomore year at the university."

"Where did you do it with her?"

"Her family had a beach house on the bay below Annapolis. We would drive down there at night."

"What did your mother say about her?"

"I don't think my mother knew about her—not from me, anyway. I never told her."

"You must have got in quite late."

"I lived at the fraternity house."

"Who was number three?"

"A woman quite a lot older than I was, while I was studying for my doctorate. She was a graduate student, too. The subject of marriage came up, but she began getting on my nerves. After she wound up her year, she went back to Chicago and married a guy out there, head of some research bureau."

"Got on your nerves? How?"

"Does it matter?"

"If I knew how she did, I might manage not to."

"It was over my dissertation. She didn't accept the idea I had for it."

"What was it about?"

"Shakespeare's sonnets."

"What was it about them that she wouldn't accept? We studied them at Delaware. I thought they were wonderful."

"When I'd worked on them awhile, I got a creepy feeling, as though the words weren't just words, but a kind of scrim, with someone back of it, talking, someone I could hear but couldn't see. Suddenly I knew who it was: a boy, a brilliant, gifted boy who was writing these things—not all of them, of course, but the 154 in the Thorpe collection. When I got that far, some mysteries began to clear up. She wouldn't believe it, though, kept insisting that no boy could have written them. She kept saying, 'You'll make a fool of yourself.' Then things went sour."

"You make me feel creepy, too."

I ticked off a few things that tied in with what I thought, and suddenly she asked: "What mysteries?"

"Well, for one, the identity of the 'Mr. W.H.' whom Thorpe, the publisher, dedicated the collection to, as 'the true begetter of these sonnets.' It has been assumed by all scholars that this was some patron, one of the noble lords Shakespeare knew, and that possibly there was a homosexual relationship there. But if he was talking to himself, if was a youth in love with his own beauty, as revealed to him in his mirror, if this was a not unusual case of teenage narcissism, 'Mr. W.H.' might well be Will Himself."

"Well, I can believe it. What other mysteries?"

"One, mainly. The identity of the 'Dark Woman'."

"Oh that's right. *Her.*"

"If these things were the work of a boy who started perhaps at fifteen, and three years had gone by since 'first your eye I eyed,' as it says in Sonnet 104, then he's now nearly eighteen, and a big event is due in his life."

"What big event?"

"You know. Of course you do."

"His marriage, you mean?"

"His *shotgun* marriage."

"Oh, that's right. She was knocked up, but good."

"By a funny coincidence, the Dark Woman enters the picture in Sonnet 127: 'In the old age black was not counted fair—' "

" 'Or if it were, it bore not beauty's name'—Well, I'll be damned! It all comes out even!"

"Hortense, you mean you believe it?"

"Why aren't you writing this up?"

"I *did* write it up. My dissertation's about it."

"I mean, *really* write it up."

"I hadn't thought about it."

I got her to bed, and she lay a long time in my arms. When at last she stirred, she whispered: "I'm sorry, I fell asleep."

"It makes me happy that you did."

"Then act happy!"

"There's a certain preliminary—?"

"Here I come!"

8

Four days later Wilmington rang me. Richard Garrett called to say he was back from London and to ask if I could be at his office the next morning at ten o'clock. I said I could, as I'd been getting ready, using the time to good advantage. I'd wound up my academic year, met with my teaching assistants, and turned them over to Dr. Shadwell, my department head. Then I had my last class. They didn't know I was leaving, but I did, and it shook me up. They formed a line to say good-bye for the semester, the boys shaking hands and the girls giving kisses. One of them had spent the whole year showing her legs to me from the front row, and she gave me a kiss, too. I was tempted to ask her name and where she lived, but didn't. I would hear from her later.

In addition to all this, I had prepped a bit on the institute, with phone calls to federal departments, for fill-in stuff I needed, to be sharp and have it down pat when I met Mr. Garrett again. The nights I spent with Hortense. She would let herself in and we would lie in the dark, whispering.

When he called, that's what we were doing. "I dread it," I confessed to her. "I dread seeing him more than

71

anything I can remember. Know what I dread most of all?"

"Not having me along?"

"That handshake with him that I'll have to go through with. I feel like the guy in that story, an O. Henry story, I guess, who couldn't drink with the man he—"

"He what?"

"Took advantage of."

"As you took advantage of me?"

"Okay, then I did."

"The story was 'Cabbages and Kings,' and the man couldn't drink with the man he blackmailed. As you blackmailed me."

"Lady, you blackmailed yourself."

"You don't have to go, Lloyd."

"Well, I do have to if—"

"Yeah? If?"

"Look, we made a decision, and—"

That's what was said, pretty gritty if we meant it. Yet ten minutes later there we were holding close, and the next morning I left for Wilmington. Miss Immelman received me as before, ushering me into the same office and saying Mr. Garrett expected me. I walked around, so nervous that I was jittery, still thinking about that handshake. But when he came in, he waved me to a chair with a bandaged right hand, and I knew why right away. He motioned to it with his left, saying: "Jabbed it last night chopping up ice for a friend. I detest cubes, like to serve rocks in lumps; so I freeze water in containers and bang into it with a pick. But sometimes I make a mislick—which I did last night but good."

But in my secret soul I knew I wasn't the only one

worrying about that handshake, and I knew she and I weren't fooling anyone.

The seat he waved me to was beside the desk. He took the swivel chair behind it, talking about his trip and how glad he was to be back. But he didn't quite look at me, only occasionally, when he seemed to be making himself do it. Soon he blurted: "Well, let's get on. I'd say the first thing is to get it incorporated, this institute we're starting. Fortunately, Delaware makes a specialty of it, so it should be easy, with no snags. I thought the boys could drive down to Dover tomorrow and get the thing over with. I'd like you to go with them, to familiarize yourself with details and get acquainted with my staff. With incorporation out of the way we can do the actual exchange of securities—from ARMALCO to the H.G. Institute. Malcolm McDavitt is in charge of the securities for ARMALCO, and for the Institute, I've asked Sam Dent to come up. He's chief of my legal staff, but bases in Washington." I said I was at his disposal, for Dover or any place I might be needed.

He drummed on the desk with his fingers, then went on: "I think you should meet McDavitt, but I have to tell you about him so you don't think I'm nuts to have him. He's in charge of all our investments. His desk is piled high with reports. He must do something about them, because he always knows what they say. But all I see him read, and I ever see him read, is his belly button. He sits at his desk, his feet up in a chair, studying it, as his father did before him. He was my father's investment chief. This is how it works: His father, back around World War I, did his umbilical research and then, suddenly announced: 'They're lining it with concrete.'

73

"Lining what with concrete?' asked my father.

" 'The whole Mississippi Valley. They've gone nuts over flood control. We're buying Portland Cement.'

"So my father bought Portland Cement—plants in California, Indiana, and Illinois—and they made him rich. They're still making me rich. Mal frightens me a little. He says he bets on my hunches, my knowing a thing from a thing. Well"—waving a hand toward the things on the shelves—"so far it's worked. But suppose I come up with a dud. Which I *can* do, Dr. Palmer. Which I can do so easy it scares me to death."

"I'd say, no use borrowing trouble."

"It's all you *can* say. Let's go in and see Mal."

So we went in there, Garrett first knocking on a door with no name on it; and sure enough, there was a rumpled, potbellied man sitting behind a desk, his feet in a swivel chair, his fingers covering his belly, and his eyes fixed on his navel. He didn't look up when we came in. Apparently he could see out of the side of his head, as he said to Garrett: "Not ARMALCO. You transfer that stuff yourself."

"What stuff?" Mr. Garrett asked.

"The securities for this thing you've decided to back. It's not a corporate enterprise—it's your private project, and you have to endow it yourself."

"Well, yeah, that's what I meant, of course."

"You said ARMALCO would do it."

"Okay, then *I* do it."

Mr. McDavitt slid a paper across his desk, at last taking his feet down. "There's the securities I'd think would do it—give this thing, whatever it is, a nicely assorted portfolio with some growth potential and still leave you well assorted. I mean, you'll kick in with quite a few things, so you're not left lopsided.

There's a tax angle, of course. Here's a memo on that."

Garrett picked up the papers, had a look, folded them, and put them in his pocket. "This is Dr. Palmer," he said, "who'll be in charge of our institution from now on."

Mal paid no attention. He didn't even look at me. "Okay, then," Mr. Garrett said after a moment, "is that all?"

Mal didn't answer, merely hoisting his feet again and going back to his belly button. Mr. Garrett led the way out. "Five minutes from now," he whispered in the hall, "he'll call me with what he thinks of you, and I'd better listen, believe me. He didn't look at you, did he? In a pig's eye, he didn't."

Back in his office we sat down and waited. The phone on his desk tinkled, and he answered. "Thanks, Mal," he said, "it's what I wanted to know."

"He says you're okay," he murmured, hanging up.

Several minutes went by, and I realized that Mal's report and Mal's assorted memos and admonitions had been very important to Garrett.

"O.K., Dr. Palmer, let's get started. What's on *your* mind?"

I said the next step, I thought, once we were incorporated, was our application to I.R.S. for a ruling on our tax-exempt status. "It's a job for lawyers," I said. "Even so, I would have to sit in, as the nub of the matter is the supplementary outline, our bound, typewritten booklet setting forth our aims and purposes. It has to be inclusive, covering everything we may conceivably want to do, so later on, if something comes up, we don't find we've booby-trapped ourselves by leaving something out. I'm the one who knows, the only one who knows in detail, what we'll want to do and how we expect to do it. So, if Mr. Dent is to be in charge as your lawyer, you should instruct him not only to work with me but to let me pass on his booklet before he actually submits it."

Mr. Garrett made a note. "I get the point," he said. "What next, after we get our ruling? How long does it take, by the way? Or do you know?"

"No more than a week or two."

"And then what?"

"There's the question of where we set up shop. I have some ideas on that, if you'd care to hear them."

"I'm listening. Go ahead."

I said that though our headquarters should be convenient to Washington, it needn't actually be in the city. "I would think, by building a place out in the suburbs, say in Prince Georges County, we could save quite a lot of expenses—if the building were in the style of a colonial mansion, no more than three stories, we wouldn't need elevators, for example, and at the same time we'd have ample space for books, records, offices, and so on. If we harmonized it with colonial architecture—"

"With a deer park, perhaps?"

"Why not? Those miniature Indian deer would cost very little and be quite a feature, especially for children."

"Swan lake?"

"In Europe they have them."

"Box hedges?"

"They give off a beautiful smell."

"Well, you can take your deer park and swan lake and box hedges and do what you want with them. But don't ask me to come in. I hate mansions and everything connected with them. Dr. Palmer, there's more comfort, more safety, more *health*, in a modern apartment building than in all the mansions ever built. I hate swan lakes, especially. They're nothing but frog ponds, reflecting the light of the moon. Poor old John Charles Thomas. I dropped in on him once before he died, in Apple Valley, California, where he lived the last years of his life. And he was telling me about the Hollywood Bowl and how some genius had the bright idea of putting a fish pond in, between the seats and the shell. 'Maybe some fish were there,' John Charles said, 'but all you could hear was frogs. I'd hate to tell you what they did to *me* one night. That's nice, isn't it? You're singing The Trumpeter, you hold the last verse, and then you start it. You breathe it at them, you've got them. You finish, and there comes that moment you pray for, of utter, reverent silence before the applause breaks out. Then a goddam frog goes *glk.*' "

"All right, the mansion is out."

"Why not a couple of floors in the Garrett Building? The one I already have on Massachusetts Avenue—in Washington, I'm talking about."

"A little slower please. You're way ahead of me."

"I have to have this Washington branch on account of the things I sell, or my companies sell. They all involve patents, and patents have to be defended at hearings of various kinds. They also involve legislation, tariffs, authorizations of one kind or another, appropriations, and so on. All that means lawyers, lobbyists, agents, gumshoes, goons, and God-knows-what. They have to have offices with phones, secretaries, and messengers. So I bought this building down there, reserved two floors for them, and rented out the other floors—ten, actually. So, O.K., why can't you take two? Or three? Or however many you'll need? I'll make the building over to you. You'll rent the other floors out, and the rent you get will be a nice lift for your budget. Is that an idea or not?"

"I'm sorry, but I have to say no."

He looked very startled and stared at me for some time. After several moments, after he had said, "You quite surprise me" and in other ways betrayed that he had been set back on his heels, he finally asked: "Why do you say that?"

"It's against the law, Mr. Garrett."

"It's *what*?"

"You can't endow a foundation and then rent yourself office space. You could until recently, but they found it was being used as a loophole, some tricky angle on taxes. So Congress closed it."

"Well! Thanks for warning me." He leaned back, staring at his desk top. His chair squeaked. He pressed a button. When Miss Immelman came in, he said: "Get on this chair, will you? Have it greased or something."

"Yes, Mr. Garrett, I will."

Then to me: "What would be your idea?"

"Why—I have no idea yet. I may get one, though. Give me a little time."

"Why don't we break for lunch? I'd invite you to the apartment, but I'm expecting someone there. You'll find the hotel good—the Du Pont, I mean. Quite good, as a matter of fact. Damned good."

"The Du Pont is fine. I'll be staying there."

After lunch I said: "If you insist on downtown Washington—and though I'm caught by surpise, I have to admit it does make sense—I would say you should buy us a building, let me take two floors, and rent out

78

the rest. I wouldn't think the right place would be too hard to find."

"Okay, will you handle it?"

"I'll do my best and keep you informed."

What he meant, I wasn't quite sure of, because if finding a building for him was what he had in mind, I knew no more about buildings than a new-born grasshopper did. But that seemed to be it, and I added: "I think I should give you a weekly progress report, with discussions in between—if, as, and when."

"Where'd you get that expression—'if, as, and when'?"

"It's one my mother was fond of. Why?"

"It's one bankers use."

"She was quite a banker herself. I wouldn't say she was fond of money, but money was fond of her."

"Money's no fool."

He looked at me sharply, and from there on in, I thought his manner toward me changed.

The next day we assembled at his office for the trip down to Dover—Ned Bramwell, his top Delaware lawyer; four or five men from his office who were to sign as incorporators, and Sam Dent, chief lawyer for the entire ARMALCO outfit, who had come up from Washington. He was the pleasantest discovery of the trip. Older than me, around forty-five, I'd say, but tall, well bred and dressed—definitely my kind of guy. We took to each other at once, but from the look on his face when the Institute was mentioned, I knew he had pretty well guessed the relationship between its patron saint and the man who was going to direct it.

We drove to Dover in two cars, I in the front seat with Dent in his car, the two youngest men from the office in back, and the rest in Bramwell's car. The whole process took no more than an hour as we moved from office to office in the capitol, signing and shuffling papers. Once there was a slip I had to sign, which I did. Then we had a late lunch. Bramwell took his gang off, and Dent and I had a long drink and talk. It turned out that he had seen me play football. We drove back to Wilmington and he dropped me off at the Du Pont. I called Mr. Garrett to ask him when he wanted to see me, but he said we were done. "However," he said, "keep in touch, will you—if, as, and when? And get on that building at once."

"I shall indeed, sir."

But my heart was already jumping with the anticipation of seeing her that night.

9

The smell of roast beef rose in my nose as soon as I unlocked the door. No light was on, but a hand raised up from behind one of the sofas and a voice said huskily: "Well, hello, hello!"

I was hungry for her. My arms ached for her, and hers went around me as I knelt to press her close, inhale her, pat her, and at last kiss her. She whispered: "We're eating in tonight—roast beef, which won't be a surprise; as you must be able to smell it. But everything else will be. I promise you, though, it will be just right for what ought to go with it."

I knew nothing to say to that except hold her closer. She moved so I could sit beside her, and then I saw the gingham apron she had on over her dress. I laughed, and she asked: "Well, what's so funny? I love you, that's all."

"It makes you look cute."

"It makes me want to snuggle."

"Okay, then snuggle."

So she snuggled and time went by. At last she drew a deep breath and said it was time to talk. "I'm so proud of you," she said.

"What have I done for you to be proud of?"

"The impression you made on *him*. He called to tell me."

"What impression?"

"You said no to him, for one thing. He's so used to yes men around him that he couldn't believe his ears at first. He was still gasping when he called me. Said you threatened to put him in jail."

"I did no such thing, and he said no such thing."

"Well, it was *something*."

"All I did was warn him that his idea was against the law."

"Yes, *that* was it."

"I said not one word about jail."

"I think that was his little joke. He has an odd sense of humor. But that wasn't all. Lloyd, you impressed him no end, the way you had done your homework, as he called it. You had things at your fingertips. Also, he says you come by your brains honest. How did your mother get in it?"

"I mentioned that money liked her."

"And he fell for her plenty."

"I happened to use an expression of hers and it seemed to catch his ear."

"What expression?"

" 'If, as, and when.' "

"Why would that catch his ear?"

"It's one bankers use."

"Oh! . . . *Oh!* Well, that *would* catch his ear."

"Speaking of ears. . . ." I began to nibble on hers, but she pushed me off.

"No, please," she said a little breathlessly. "There's more."

"Say on, pretty creature, say on."

"He was suspicious of you before—half-liked you

82

but thought you were much too cheeky to really have any brains. But your saying no to him caught his attention, and suddenly he's now sold all the way, even on you, as the person who should be in charge. Isn't that wonderful?"

"I thought I detected a change in his manner."

But I must have seemed withdrawn or hesitant or something short of joyous, because suddenly she pulled away in the dark and asked: "Well, for heaven's sake, what is it *now*?"

"It doesn't quite add up."

"What doesn't add up?"

"In the first place, he knows."

"Lloyd, how could he possibly know?"

"How could he possibly not?"

"Then, O.K., he knows. But if he's sold on you even *when* he knows, what is there to have a long face about?"

"I told you—it doesn't add up." I told her about the hand he had injured, and she jumped up, all excited.

"But he *does* chop ice! He never uses cubes."

"O.K., but then he switched."

"I told you he did. He *explained* it."

"Yeah, but in regard to *you*—"

"It's simple, if you just remember that he loves me—all except in that one, just that one, way. So if he thought you were kind of a phoney and very bad for me, it could account for the first way he felt, even including that hand, if that's the reason he had, though he told me about it, about jabbing it with the ice pick, I mean—and he wouldn't have, if it was just something he made up and put the bandage on to pretend. So, at first, he was upset on my account, and then he wasn't. It could be as simple as that."

"Wait a minute. Maybe that makes sense."

I didn't know whether it did or not, but at least I felt that it could—and anything to please her after her sweet, romantic welcome. I kissed her and pretty soon she kissed back. "I think the roast is done," she said.

Is there any greater intimacy than a man frying eggs for his woman or her roasting beef for him? Once more we were there at the kitchen table, she letting me carve, then serving me vegetables, the boiled new potatoes with parsley butter on them and the peas on little glass plates. We gobbled our dinner down, now and then touching cheeks, and I told her how happy I was. But in the still of the night, she whispered: "I almost forgot. He's bringing Inga back, which, in a way, is the best news of all."

"Who's Inga?"

"I told you—the Swedish housekeeper we had, who got a cable from Stockholm while I was in the hospital with my miscarriage. He had to pack her off, but now he's bringing her back."

"Why is that good news?"

"It has to mean he's getting organized to live alone."

"Leaving us a clear track, you mean?"

She burrowed close, and for some time nothing was said. But I knew she wasn't asleep.

"Lloyd, there's just one thing."

"What is it, Hortense?"

"Listen, do you or don't you?"

"Do I or don't I what?"

"Love me?"

"You know I do."

I threw back the covers, flopped her over, and fanned her backside until it sounded like pistol shots in

84

the dark. Then her arms were wrapped around my neck.

"I'm a degenerate," she said. "I love it when you bop me."

10

My finding a building was purely by accident, and I got credit for brains I didn't have. One day I woke up with a drawstring on my stomach—from the fact that I had a job to do and no idea how to do it. Hortense gave me my breakfast, there-thered me, and promised between kisses that something was bound to turn up. I called her Mrs. Micawber. She said: "Instead of glooming about it and feeling sorry for yourself, you could make some use of the day, like paying a courtesy call on Ralph—Ralph Hood, the senator. Except for writing him a note, which really isn't much, you've done nothing about him. Why don't you take him to lunch? Or at least *invite* him?"

So I called his office and a bit to my surprise got through to him at once. He said he'd check his calendar and see if he was free and call me back. He did, and he was free. I said I would pick him up in my car, as the only place I was known was at Harvey's, and from his office, it would be too far to walk. He told me to put my car in a parking lot and he would "blow" me to the ride.

At twelve I stopped by his office and for twenty minutes had to shake hands and chat with the admin-

istrative assistant, the assistant assistants, and the secretaries—all in the outer office. Then for ten minutes I
was admitted to his private office where the decorations consisted of framed pictures of him shaking
hands with presidents Kennedy and Johnson, with the
Queen of England, and with Smokey the Bear. At last
we went downstairs. The guard at the door said to
him: "Your car is waiting, Senator." And sure enough,
it was—at the curb, a Chrysler limousine with uni-
formed driver. We chatted as we rode, and I gave him
the big piece of news, that the Institute seemed to be
set, "and it's all due to you, Senator. I can't thank you
enough."

He held up a hand. "I like to be thanked, but it was
due to you, not me. I've heard a little about it. Richard
Garrett called me, and so did Hortense. You impressed him no end—and her even more, I suspect.
Lloyd, I wasn't surprised. You impressed me, too, in
court that day. More important, you impressed the
judge. I would even go so far as to say that you set him
back on his heels somewhat."

This left me slightly crossed up, that this reaction to
me, Mr. Garrett's reaction, I mean, which he had
passed on to her by phone, had now become official.
So it was being passed on to everyone. But I began to
realize that it was the only reaction that could be
maintained. If I was a guy whose wife would shortly
be paired more or less publicly with the head of an
institute he was underwriting, the only way he could
play it would be straight, make noises that this friend
of his wife's was really some kind of genius, that Dr.
Palmer had the job for *that* reason and not for reasons
that might be inferred. But, of course, I said nothing
about this to the senator. I merely listened while he

talked on.

When we arrived at Harvey's, which is a basement restaurant with underground parking for cars, I gave the driver ten dollars to go have his lunch. Then I led the way to my table which I had reserved by phone and which the girl, a rather good-looking maitresse d', had waiting when we got there. We ordered, and when Senator Hood asked for a martini, so did I. He resumed discussing the Institute and the future I could look forward to, "now that the Garretts have fallen for you." But I must not have been paying attention, because he stopped in midsentence and asked: "What is it, Lloyd? What did I say?"

"It's not you, Senator; it's him. Mr. Garrett."

"Lloyd, he's big."

"He's been stuck with me, once I got her on my side, but he keeps blowing me up, making me bigger than I am. It makes me damned uneasy. A person knows his limitations."

"Maybe he's *not* blowing you up. You impressed me just as much as you apparently did him. That ghastly day in court, when you calmly took charge up there on the witness stand and got it into the record that the pot they found in Jack's car must have been planted by the police, which, you thought, was most unlikely, or else stashed by someone else because it was hot and had to be gotten rid of, as to your certain knowledge that it was not in the glove compartment when you and the boys left the car to go to the basketball game. It was a cool, nervy performance, your making that judge listen, and once he listened, *believe*. It was a day I'll never forget. So I'm not so sure that Richard Garrett overrates you. Perhaps, as they say, you don't know your own strength."

Though I certainly didn't mean to, I had sounded cranky, so I started kidding along with the waitress as a way to save face. When she left again, the senator asked: "Lloyd, something's bugging you more than you've been letting on. Come on, what is it? If you want to talk, that is."

I didn't want to, but I could hardly help it. I blurted out the whole thing—about the building, the law against renting yourself office space, which, it turned out, he had voted for, being ordered to find a building and soon. Senator Hood began to laugh.

"It's like being given a scuba outfit and told to find the lost Atlantis," he said. "And it also sounds like Richard Garrett, who is in the habit of commanding things to be done forthwith, and then, presto whango, they are . . . sometimes." Suddenly the grin left his face, as though Marcel Marceau had waved his hand across it, and he started snapping his finger at the girl. "Miss," he said when she sashayed over, "I'm Senator Hood of Nebraska, and something has come up. We have to leave. We'll be gone about a half-hour. When we come back, we will want our lunch ready exactly as we ordered it. Keep our table for us, please."

"Yes, sir," she said as he pressed a bill in her hand.

"What is it, Senator?" I asked, wondering if he were ill.

"You'll see. Come on, Lloyd."

We went upstairs and out on the street. A taxi stopped for us as soon as he had raised his hand. He gave an address on K Street, and when we got there he told the driver to park, "here by the curb—we want to sit for a minute and then go back where we came from." Through the window he pointed at the building across the street. It was still under construction.

Scaffolding was all around it and out over the sidewalk. It was a beautiful modern thing of sandstone. But it wasn't one of those buildings that look like a refrigerator with windows cut in the sides. It had windows, of course, but they were spaced in a graceful way, with stone in between. I counted ten floors. The top two were set back in a kind of mansard style, a little like the Lincoln Memorial. The entrance was beautiful—no columns, no fancy stuff, just two large bronze doors. He stared and then said quietly: "How would that do for your institute?"

"Perfect! Wonderful!"

"Let's go back to Harvey's, driver."

While we rode, he talked. "You've heard of Bagastex?"

"I've heard of bagasse."

"That's right—Bagastex is made of bagasse—that stuff they get when they grind the juice out of sugarcane. It's a floor covering that was developed by the Tombigvannah Corporation in Georgia. They tooled up, spent millions on it, and put up that building there, the one you just looked at. They had it made, they thought. By the end of the year they were due to line up with the big ones. And then the boom got lowered. Bagastex didn't sell. Meanwhile, in Georgia they had had the bad judgment to fudge on their taxes. They knew they could be heading for trouble but figured that with the money they'd be making, they could square up and get on with the show without being caught. But they couldn't. And they can't meet their installment here, their last one on the building, with the contractor. So tomorrow in court the contractor will sue to have them declared bankrupt so their assets can be impounded and their creditors paid—perhaps. How do I know this? A certain senator came to me for help in getting a postponement tomorrow. But I can't do a thing. There are reasons why I simply don't dare to. But *you* can do something. You can phone Richard Garrett and have him get on it quick. It's the chance of a lifetime, to pick up a building dirt cheap and perhaps do more than that. So, get on it. But remember: *keep me out of it!*?"

"I hear you, Senator. O.K."

Back at Harvey's, he paid for the cab. When we returned to our table, the maitresse d' was there, looking at her watch.

"You were gone twenty-five minutes," she said to the senator. "I'll tell teacher to give you an apple."

"Honey, I love you," he told her.

He had her bring a phone and phone box, and we looked the numbers up, especially Tombigvannah's lawyer, a man named Downing, who had offices in the Pell Building on Fourteenth Street. I wrote everything down on the four-by-six cards a researcher invariably carries and finally put in a call to Wilmington. Miss Immelman transferred my call to Mr. Garrett's office. He was friendly and interested in what I was calling about. "It's a beautiful thing," I assured him and described the building. "It's really something. How much of it I'll need, I don't know right now—two floors at least, perhaps three. But the other floors, you can rent out." But when I tried to explain the deal and mentioned Tombigvannah, he cut in quickly and hard.

"I know all about that. They've been propositioning me about Bagastex for a couple of years at least, and, of course, I've had it looked into. But the next question concerns *you*. What's your connection with it?"

"I don't have any connection."

"Where'd you get your information?"

"That, I'm not free to divulge, Mr. Garrett."

"Dr. Palmer, I have to know."

"Why?"

"For one thing, there can be no secrets between us—not on this can there be. And for another, I have to be sure you're not being used as a catspaw."

"A what?"

"A means to an end."

"You mean, I could have been fed this tip as bait, so I would pass it on to you, and—"

"Exactly."

"I assure you, it's nothing like that."

"You *think* it's nothing like that."

When I hung up, the senator, who had heard, shook his head gloomily. "I'm sorry, Lloyd," he said, "but I had to sew it up. I couldn't help it. There are things I can't go into. It could cost me my seat to get mixed up in this mess. . . . Well, thanks for standing pat. I'd have expected it of you. Can't say more than that."

The food came and I ordered a bottle of Chablis, but he said: "Make it a split." When the waitress brought it, she also brought the phone back, saying: "Long-distance call, Dr. Palmer. My, but you're busy today."

It was Mr. Garrett again. When I expressed surprise that he knew where I was, he said: "I called Hortense to find out what she knew, and she didn't know anything except where you were and who with—which, of course, cleared up one thing right away. But while I was talking to her, Miss Immelman brought me the file, the stuff I have on Bagastex, and right now I'm looking at a memo I hadn't seen before which makes it a whole new ball game—and how. So, Lloyd, once again, you've done it. Now let me talk to the senator."

I hesitated a moment and then said: "I'll see if he's still here."

Cupping my hand over the phone, I said to Senator Hood: "Do you want to talk to him? He found out I'm with you, from Hortense."

"O.K., Paul Pry," the senator said, taking the phone; "I'll give you what help I can. But don't quote me and don't record this call. Is the bug on or off? . . . O.K., what do you want to know?"

He answered questions in a quick, straight-from-the-shoulder way, and I got a glimpse of the enormous body of knowledge a big shot has to have to be a big shot. I also got a glimpse of one of the crookedest deals I've ever heard of—a scheme with forty angles, to defraud investors, growers, creditors, contractors, machinery manufacturers, and the government. I understood at last why he couldn't get mixed up in it. Finally he was done and handed the phone back to me.

"Lloyd," Mr. Garrett said in a very friendly tone; "you did the right thing in protecting the senator until he chose to break silence. On that part, no hard feelings. I'll be down in a couple of hours to look this building over, and if I like it, I'll move in—or try to. So will you stand by at home for my call in case I need you? And will you tell Hortense I'm on my way?"

"You want this dope I have? The lawyer and so on?"

"I'll have Miss Immelman take it."

I got home around three and called Hortense. I told her that Garrett was on his way to Washington, but that left us dangling. We would have to stand by as we were, with no idea when we could see each other, and especially *whether* we could. But we had reached the point where we hungered for those nights, and I told her: "I feel funny inside, as though a vacuum were there."

"You always say it exactly the way I feel it. It would look peculiar, though, if I weren't here when he arrives."

"You have to be there, of course."

So we sweated it out. But around five he called me to say that he was at the Garrett Building and to meet him at Downing's office. I drove in. The Pell Building is on Fourteenth Street below H Street, and I put the car in a New York Avenue parking lot and walked. But who did I meet, also walking, but Mr. Garrett! He waved and fell in step beside me. But he didn't shake hands. At Downing's office the girls had gone.

"We have the place to ourselves," Downing said. He was a man around forty, slightly bald, and most deferential to Mr. Garrett, telling him: "Sir, you may not remember me, but I met you once, and I've heard you speak once or twice. I was the one on the front row, taking notes."

"Yes, I remember you well," said Mr. Garrett.

We laughed, and Mr. Garrett introduced me. "Dr. Palmer will sit in on this," he said.

"Not with me, he won't," Downing said. "No one sits in on this but thee and me, Mr. Garrett."

"Oh? You've got to that certain point?"

"What certain point?"

"Of excluding all witnesses."

"Okay, call it that."

They went into Downing's private office while I tramped around the reception room and outer offices, the doors of which were open. I examined the big framed portraits of Roger Taney, Charles Evans Hughes, William Howard Taft, Earl Warren, and Warren Burger until I knew practically every fold of their robes. I did this for an hour. Every so often the snarl of Downing's voice told me there might be a reason for excluding witnesses. Later, I found out that what the argument was about was what had been done by Colonel Lucas, the president of Tombigvannah when Bagastex began to sag. He had sold off Tombig subsidiaries, ostensibly for cash to operate with but actually to detach them from the crash when it came, so they would stay in the Lucas family, as the buyer was Lucas's brother.

Garrett, while offering a decent deal—cash to the building contractor and ARMALCO stock for Tombig, on a three-for-one basis—was doing it only on the condition that Tombig recaptured the subsidiaries and bought them back for what had been paid. They included a cigar factory in Charleston, a breakfast food plant in Savannah, a lumber mill in Alabama, and a power plant near Augusta. The recapture stipulation was what Downing was snarling about. But Mr. Garrett didn't snarl. He didn't have to. He was holding trump cards, as he usually did. As a sort of preliminary to whatever might come up, he had bought stock some time before—Tombig stock—and he now told Downing: "O.K., we let the bankruptcy suit proceed, if that's how you want to play it. But this afternoon or tomorrow, a stockholder who happened to buy in just in case, will file a complaint alleging fraudulent disposal of assets before involuntary bankruptcy, which is a felony. And if Leonard Downing's a party to it, if it turns out that he helped compound the fraud, something very unpleasant is going to happen to Leonard Downing."

"I see. I see."

So that's how things stood—at least as I piece them together now from what was told me later—when Mr. Garrett came out, closed the door, and dialed one of the secretary's phones, still without looking at me. In a moment he began to talk in a low, guarded tone: "Sam?"—who seemed to be Sam Dent, my friend from the Dover trip—"Sam, I'm at a lawyer's office, man named Leonard Downing, in the Pell Building. I need you here at once. Yes, it's on that Tombigvannah thing."

He hung up and then sat down in a chair, still paying no attention to me. Pretty soon Downing came out, half-sat on the typewriter table, and mopped his bald spot with his handkerchief. "Well," he said, "we're in luck. Colonel Lucas is on his way over. He just happened to be in town."

"I thought he might be," said Mr. Garrett.

"We could wind this thing up tonight."

"I just talked to Sam Dent, my lawyer. He's on his way."

"Yeah, I know Sam."

They paid no attention to me then or when various people arrived, in gabardines, summer suits, and shorts. Downing would jerk his thumb as soon as a new one showed, and he would join the others in one of the inner offices. Then a big, heavyset man came in. He had that brown mahogany color that stays outdoors all the time. His name, I later learned, was O'Connor. He was the contractor. Downing introduced him to Mr. Garrett, saying: "This is *the* Richard

Garrett, Jim. We're trying to lay a deal—a three-way thing for cash, stock, and assets—that will clear up things for you. So act respectful."

"I would, anyway."

"Okay, but lean on it."

"Mr. Garrett, greetings, sir."

"Jim, I've heard of you, and nothing but good."

Then Sam Dent came in, and Mr. Garrett at once took him into one of the offices to talk. But when they came out, he looked worried. Then at last came a character who had to be seen to be believed, and even then he didn't look real. He was about fifty, with white hair, white eyebrows, and white goatee, as well as a white sharkskin suit, white shoes, and an old-fashioned Panama hat, and he carried a gold-headed cane. Here was the genuine article, a Southern colonel with so much honesty shining out of his face that I wouldn't have trusted him—and no sensible person would—any farther than I could throw him.

"Colonel Lucas," exclaimed Downing, first bowing and then shaking hands; "I give you Mr. Richard Garrett, *the* Mr. Richard Garrett!"

"Mr. Garrett," said the colonel, "the pleasure of this moment is surpassed only by its memorable nature, from the honor it accords me." Or "accowds me," actually, to report it as it sounded.

"Colonel Lucas," said Mr. Garrett, "I reciprocate the sentiments you express, if not in such felicitous words, then in equal uplift of spirit. I have long looked forward to this honor."

His face was also glowing with honesty—or, at least, with something. The two men went into Downing's office, closed the door, and left the rest of us to twiddle our thumbs. Dent came over, and we shook

98

hands. "Will you be seeing Mrs. Garrett soon?" he said. "Like, for instance, tonight?"

"I hadn't expected to. Why?"

"He pays attention to what she says. You could put the bug in her bonnet to talk him out of this thing."

"You mean Bagastex?"

"Yeah, Bagastex."

"But what do I know about it? And what do you?"

"I know plenty about it."

He started talking about how Bagastex had flopped and how ARMALCO was heading for trouble in loading itself down with such a headache. I interrupted to say that I was partly responsible, since I had tipped Mr. Garrett off to the deal, and besides, I felt that it tied in with the Institute I was starting. Sam kept shaking his head, but then the door of Downing's office flew open and there was the colonel, his hat in one hand and his cane in the other, his hair falling down on his shoulders. "Sir," he bellowed back toward the office, "what do you take me for? That you would insult me so?" Mr. Garrett strolled out, cool, calm, and friendly. "Colonel," he said quietly, "I take you for a peach, a beautiful Georgia peach that's been skinned, the slipperiest object yet created by God. You *are* beautiful. You *are* skinned. Bagastex saw to that. And you *are* slippery. That, you have to admit."

"I do not admit any such thing. And I resent your remowk."

"I was just being funny."

"I see nothing funny about it."

"*Trying* to be funny, let us say."

"I demand an apowlogy from you."

"I apologize."

"What has been said is not so easily unsaid."

"It's the insidious way I work."

"Then you still mean that I am 'slippery'?"

"I still mean that you were skinned—by Bagastex, its investors, and all the investors' friends. I still mean that you are broke and had better make a deal before the government takes you to the cleaners. I still mean enough cash to bail you out—of the building, on a three-for-one stock deal that will give you something to fall back on, and your retirement as president of Tombigvannah."

"It is that condition, sir, which I regowd as an insult."

"A compliment, you should call it. In my company, I'm the big bull elephant. You may not see the tusks—"

"I feel them, sir, in my ribs."

"And in *your* company, you're the bull. But there's no room for two big bulls in an elephant herd. One of us has to give ground. So—"

He didn't finish. Flinging his hat and cane on the typewriter table and slumping into the secretary's chair, the colonel collapsed in tears, dropping his head on his chest and sobbing uncontrollably.

Downing turned to O'Connor with a gesture that meant things were settled. At first O'Connor looked surprised, but then he nodded. Mr. Garrett put his arm around the colonel and said to Sam Dent: "Get it on paper."

"Mr. Garrett," sobbed the colonel, "I truly thank you."

"My privilege, sir; I assure you."

The two of them followed Downing and Sam into Downing's office and the door closed behind them.

The thing went on for an hour, with Downing at last popping out, a pencil between his teeth, to open the typewriter desk, put in paper with carbons, and begin pecking away, while Mr. Garrett and Sam Dent took turns popping out, whispering in Downing's ear, and laying yellow legal pad worksheets beside him. Pretty soon Downing took the stuff he had typed back to his office, then came back out and closed the desk.

"Christ, what a night!" he said and started into his office again. But at that moment the outer door opened, and Hortense was standing there in a dark dress and green coat. Everyone seemed to know who she was and jumped up respectfully. They seemed almost excited. She saw me and waved a friendly, if baffled, greeting. Downing did it big, introducing himself and telling her: "Mr. Garrett's in my office, Mrs. Garrett. He asked you to come down so you could look at a building he expects to acquire."

"Oh, *that!*"

"He's right in there."

But before Downing could escort her in, the door opened and Mr. Garrett, Dent, and the colonel came out. Each of them had a piece of typewritten paper and they all acted friendly. When Mr. Garrett saw Hortense he kissed her and said how pretty she looked, which caused twinges to go through me. He let her say hello to Sam and then presented the colonel whose finest hour it now turned out to be. He bent over, kissed her hand, and said: "Mrs. Garrett, the honor, the privilege, the thrill I feel at last, to meet a lady I have heard about, every word of it praise, completely overwhelms me."

Hortense dropped a curtsey, crossing her hands on her heart and bowing low. "Colonel Lucas," she said, "the honor is mine. I'll cherish its memory always."

She straightened up, and Mr. Garrett gave it a hand, which I wished he hadn't done; it made her curtsey seem phoney. He said: "Hortense, I thought before things are made final tomorrow, you would like to look at the building I've bought, the one Dr. Palmer picked for your institute."

"Tonight? Just like that?"

"Well, why not?"

"It's an odd time to be taking a look, but—"

"It's only nine o'clock."

"Then let's get it over with. Who are these gentlemen?"

He introduced them, and I could see her, out of force of habit, memorizing the names. Then we all went out into the hall, piled into an elevator, and went downstairs. We had to take three cabs to the building. When Hortense, Mr. Garrett, and I arrived, O'Connor was there ahead of us, waiting with the watchman and his flashlight to show us through. But Mr. Garrett had the cab stop across the street. When he pointed to the building, Hortense caught her breath. "It's beautiful, just beautiful," she said reverently. And it certainly was. By moonlight, it showed up gray and ghostly, its proportions even more striking than they had been by day.

We got out of the cab and crossed the street, and O'Connor took us through it. We used the one elevator that was in service. O'Connor took us upstairs and down again, finally showing us the "stockbrokers' board room," as he called it, across from the elevators downstairs. But Hortense corrected him.

"Mr. O'Connor," she said, "it may have been designed for eminent stockholders, but now it has become the reception room of the Hortense Garrett Biographical Institute, and for that purpose, is perfection itself. Do you agree, Dr. Palmer?"

"I can't imagine anything better."

And I couldn't. It was large, a bit higher than most rooms and wainscotted in some kind of wood. It was dignified in a quiet, high-toned way.

A half-hour later we were in the Black Tahiti Restaurant just down the street. We all ordered margaritas and some sort of Polynesian food which I don't remember the name of, but Hortense was the only one who had anything to eat. When the drinks came, Garrett tasted the salt on his glass, raised it, and said: "To the Hortense Garrett Institute." When we had all taken a sip, he added: "Once more Dr. Palmer reaches out and grabs the brass ring from nowhere."

"Dr. Palmer," I said, "did nothing of the sort. He just passed on a tip that paid off—as we think."

"I imagine you saw, though, after meeting the colonel, Lloyd, why I had to be sure you weren't being used?"

"Was he using *you* is the question," Sam Dent said.

103

I should have been pleased with myself, but I wasn't. We were in a booth. I don't know whether the Garretts being on one side of the table, with Dent and me on the other, upset me or what; but for some reason I felt gloomy in spite of the building and the giant steps we were taking toward getting the Institute started. But Sam was truly depressed.

"The point," he said, "is not the brass ring that was grabbed or who was using whom, but what we do with the worst turkey I ever heard of, now that we seem to have it. Mr. Garrett, I hate to be a killjoy, but if Bagastex broke Colonel Lucas, think what it will do to you."

"Make me rich is all."

"Richer," Hortense said. "He's already filthy rich— except that the Hortense Garrett Institute will, to some extent, change that situation."

"How can stuff you can't sell make you rich?" Sam asked.

"By my changing the angle of promotion."

"Lucas gave it all the promotion a product could ask for. That's what landed him behind the eight ball."

"I said I would change the angle."

"Am I supposed to ask how?"

"By ninety degrees, exactly."

"What is this, some kind of joke?"

"Not at all, Sam. As you've observed a great many times, Bagastex, horizontal, was a flop, a turkey, a bust. It had to be made too thick. Kids tripped on it. It took a power tool to cut it. And it created a storage problem in places that handled it. But *vertical*—as house siding—it's perfect. That's where the ninety degrees come in. I had some of the stuff sent to the lab up in Wilmington and told them to work on it, see what it was good for, if anything. Don't forget, Sam, I often know a thing from a thing, and with this crazy thing, the point of it is: it's cheap. So they heated it, hoping it would soften and they could press a matrix into it and mold it to look like bricks or stone or something. But all it did was turn white. No matter what color it had been from the dye that had been put in it, when it was heated, it turned white. Pete Holton there in the lab kept thinking there had to be some way of making use of that characteristic. And all of a sudden, he had it— or thought he had. He loaded some oil bidons on a truck, drove down to Georgia, and propositioned the Bagastex foreman for a few gallons to take back home so he could fill up that hole in his cellar without calling a goddam plumber who would, in turn, have to apply for a permit which he wasn't at all sure he could get because it involved his sewer connection. So, for a hundred bucks, the foreman filled the bidons with liquid Bagastex, the mush they rolled into sheets and tried to sell as linoleum. It just so happened that this batch of stuff was red, so when Pete got back, he poured a bidon of it into the tray he'd used for heating, and as it was starting to set, he pressed a matrix into it, one he'd made from a brick wall, a hammered mold of wet cardboard that he had let dry. The Bagastex took the impression and looked exactly like brick except that the joints were red, just like the rest. But a hot wire grid, when he pressed it down on them, burned them white; they looked like the plaster between bricks. Then he built a small house of the stuff on the hill there by the lab. He's been swamped with inquiries about it. Curiously, it uncorked one advantage we hadn't anticipated, that no metal siding has. It's slightly porous, so ivy clings to it, which it won't do to steel, aluminum, or copper."

"I just love that little brick privy," murmured Hortense with stars in her eyes—"its walls all covered with ivy—"

"You go wash your mouth out with soap," Mr. Garrett snapped.

"I'm showing appreciation!"

He tried to reprove her some more but had to laugh in spite of himself. We all had to laugh.

Mr. Garrett went on: "The funny part of it was that I knew nothing about it until Lloyd Palmer called. Holton had sent me a memo, but I didn't take time to read it until Miss Immelman brought me the file we had on Bagastex. There it was on top—and I got busy quick. So . . . once more we have Lloyd Palmer to thank. Let's drink to him."

By then more margaritas had been ordered. They all picked theirs up, and I picked mine up before I remembered that I shouldn't drink. By now I thought it was impossible to feel any crummier, in spite of the laughing I'd done. But with those three glasses raised in my honor, I managed it. Garrett looked at his watch and then asked Sam if he was all squared away for tomorrow.

"I am," Dent said, "if Mrs. G. likes the building and you've come to a final decision that you want the deal to go through."

"I love it," Hortense said.

"Then it's all yours, Sam. See that O'Connor is paid, and for God's sake, check all the stock that Lucas turns in for those subsidiary companies. I don't say he'd forge duplicates—"

"*I* do."

106

"Let's both say it, then."

"Mr. Garrett, it's all under control."

"O.K., take it away."

Mr. Garrett looked at his watch, motioned to the waitress for the check, then got up and followed her to the desk to pay it. When he came back, Sam asked him: "You'll be here tomorrow?"

"I hadn't expected to be. I have to be getting back. If something comes up, call me and—"

"You're going back tonight?" Hortense asked, surprised.

"It's not too late. I'll have the road to myself."

"Well, don't wake me by calling me up."

"Do I ever? How did you get here, by the way?"

"Taxi."

"Lloyd, would you see her home?"

"Be only too glad, of course."

Mr. Garrett had left his car in the ARMALCO garage. As soon as we were out on the street, he flagged a cab to take him there. He kissed Hortense, got in, and drove off. Same Dent flagged a cab, kissed her, and drove off. By then, I had told her where I was parked, but without saying a word, we knew we weren't calling a cab. We swung hands and started walking down Seventeenth Street by the light of the moon, carefree, goofy, and happy just from knowing we would be together that night. We hardly said anything driving out or in the apartment, hanging her coat up, or having our first kiss of the evening.

She insisted on scrambling some eggs, "because you didn't have much to eat, and I love cooking for you." So we ate her little supper, went to bed, and for awhile were close. Then, stretched out on top of me, she

107

whispered: "Did you hear what he said? 'Lloyd, will you see her home?' *This* is my home."

"Well, except for the wall decorations, it—"

"The stomach, not the apartment!"

"Oh. Then, it has a beautiful tenant."

"Tenant?"

"Well—mate."

"Wife, I think you mean."

"I wish I did, but I don't. You have a husband already."

"You're the only husband I have or ever expect to have."

"I tell it like it is."

She rolled off me, and I said: "However, I love you."

"Then act like it."

I acted like it, and after some time, she was topside again, kissing my neck.

12

In Wilmington, Washington, and various places, things now began to accelerate. Next in our order of business was the application we had made to I.R.S. for a tax-exempt status. To sit in with us on that, Sam brought in a tax lawyer, a character named Kaufman, who was a bit of a stuffed shirt, but was a shark on tax law, which was what we hired him for. Around Sam's age, he was grossly overweight. Kaufman insisted that we work in his office on Sixteenth and C because his reference books were there, so I would walk there every day from the Garrett Building on Massachusetts. The reason I had to sit in was that I knew what the Institute would be doing. So day after day, for the supplemental booklet we would submit, I dictated to Kaufman's secretary a detailed account of our projected activities, so every possible thing would be covered and we wouldn't hit any snags later just by failing to include some material in our application—"to acquire, repair, and shelve books, pamphlets, periodicals, manuscripts, and source material of all kinds"; "to employ researchers, technicians, scholars, consultants, and librarians for the assistance of scholars writing biography or writing anything which, in the judgment of the director, contributes to biographical study"; "to employ persons qualified to prepare indices for the assistance of scholars writing biography"; "to acquire, operate, and maintain recorders and employ technicians to maintain them, such recorders to use film, tape, wax, wire, or other means of reproduction, oral or visual or both, for the preservation of biographical material"—and so on for eighty-five pages in blue cover, until my tongue had kinks in it from dictating such gobbledygook. But Kaufman seemed satisfied, and it was Garrett who called at nine-thirty one morning while Hortense was still in bed to tell me: "Lloyd, I've just opened my mail and wanted you to be the first one to know. We have our ruling."

"We have our—"

"Ruling. From I.R.S. We're in."

"Well, hey, that's wonderful news. I'd heard they were fairly prompt but didn't expect action so soon. It's hardly been a week."

"Our application's in order and on the up and up, that's why. Kaufman gives you full credit—while, of course, saving some for himself."

"He did fine. Well, I'm pleased."

That put him up tight and me up tight—him because by now rumors were going around, with stuff coming out in the papers, and he had to make some kind of announcement, and me because I was named in the rumors and the university kept calling me, especially the president's office, to know what was going on and whether I would be there next year, as so far I hadn't resigned, not being quite sure how things would finally turn out. So I had to make up my mind, and did.

110

In a short, hand-written note, I resigned. Mr. Garrett had also made up his mind. He asked me to come up to discuss his press statement. So next morning I was in his Wilmington office, listening to his idea on how to make the announcement. It was weird, to say the least but at the same time, interesting, because it showed how little a big wheel understands public relations or what he owes the public in the way of information. He thought it was enough to send out a brochure, one I would write, "of two thousand words or so," describing the Institute, along with an engraved announcement, "and that's all. I've checked off the newspapers here that I think the brochure should go to."

He had his thumb marking a place in a book, which he passed to me. It was Ayer's newspaper directory. He had put markers in for Boston, New York, Philadelphia, Baltimore, Washington, Norfolk, Richmond, and a few more places, with check marks beside the big papers in each city, which you couldn't overlook, of course, as the circulation figures told you. I glanced at it here and there, and while I did this, he went on: "I may say that, since this is in my wife's honor, for once in her life, I don't want her besmirched—by printer's ink, I mean—as she has been in Wilmington. After all, it's a private matter, and when we've come up with all legitimate information. I think we should cut it off. I think we're *entitled* to cut it off."

"Private? Cut what off? I don't understand."

"Well, isn't it? It's my money."

"It's your money, but you're claiming exemption from taxes. That makes it public."

"I hadn't thought of it that way."

"As far as Mrs. Garrett goes, I don't believe for one

second that she minded very much, that she really minded at all, the things that came out in the papers, especially the pictures. In plain English, she loved it. This idea you seem to have, of cheating her out of her big moment, strikes me as somewhat silly."

"Well, thanks."

"You're welcome."

"What's your idea about it?"

"My idea is: maybe the press isn't perfect, but they're the only press we have, so if we can't lick 'em, let's join 'em. They're there, and it's up to us whether they tell it our way or some other cockeyed way that needn't have happened at all, if we'd just got with it and played our cards right."

"You mean, stacked the deck?"

"Okay, what's wrong with stacking it?"

"How *do* we stack it, then?"

"The announcement, the brochure, and the mailing list are fine as far as they go. Count on me to fix up the style. But we should also get out a press release, a Xerox job that we write up ourselves, with names, dates, places, and a release date—all complete."

"What names, besides my wife's?"

"Our governing board, for one thing."

"It hasn't even been appointed."

"No, but I've picked the nominees." I took out my list of historians, biographers, librarians, university department heads, and financial bigwigs, and passed it over to him. "They should be queried," I said. "And when we have their acceptances—"

"They're probably on vacation now."

"They can be reached by phone—or rather, most of them can."

"Okay, I'll begin calling today."

112

"*I'll* begin calling today."

"What's your objection to me?"

He seemed startled, so I told him: "*I'm* the director. Or am I?"

"Of course you are, Lloyd."

"Then I'll call."

"Fine."

He stared for a moment and then asked: "And what places?"

"The location of the press conference you should hold, as the host graciously answering any questions that may come up."

"That's more up my wife's alley."

"I was going to suggest that you ask her to arrange it."

"All right, what else?"

"That's all I can think of right now."

Hortense arranged it at one of Washington's big hotels, with me sitting in as a sort of advisor, but not until she had "a few minutes alone with Monsieur Pierre, Dr. Palmer." That seemed to mean money was going to change hands. By the time I got back, Monsieur Pierre was purring out loud. He was a sleek-looking guy with an accent I didn't quite place. He set it up exactly as she wanted—for Conference Room A, with counter, bar, and buffet at one end, telephones at the other, and chairs in the middle. The only hitch came over the canapes. When she mentioned them to him, Monsieur Pierre frowned, but she told him emphatically: "I know they're a lot of trouble and that hotels hate to fool with them. But these will be newspaper people who are not only chronic freeloaders but will have their hands full of pencils, papers, cameras, tape recorders, and all sorts of things—and to expect them to scoop up dip with potato chips or spear lobster tails with a fork is not being realistic. I want to make it easy for them—dips, shrimp, lobster tails, and potato salad of course, but also, if you could stretch a point, Monsieur Pierre—"

It turned out that he could.

For my two cents worth I asked for three armchairs—"with a mike beside each—one for Mrs. Garrett, one for Mr. Garrett, and one for me, facing the rows of folding chairs. Since they will be shooting pictures of us, we should be in comfortable positions. Also, in addition to your counter, bar, and buffet, I want a decent-sized table to hold the printed matter we'll have on hand to give out. I want it put at one side near the door, so if any reporter forgets something, he can grab it on the way out."

Monsieur Pierre made a note.

She had come down in a cab. When we were through I suggested: "Why don't you come out with me? Then in the morning I'll drive you in, and—"

"I can't, Lloyd; Mother's here."

"Oh. Then invite me out. I'd like to meet her."

"That thought crossed my mind, but for some reason, I shied off."

"Okay, no use pushing our luck."

"With her, there will be plenty of time."

By the day of the news conference, stacks of material had been delivered to the apartment, not only the announcements, brochures, and releases but a couple of dozen copies of our application to I.R.S., in case some reporter wanted to cover us thoroughly. In addition, there were Xeroxed capsule biographies, mainly taken from *Who's Who in America*, of the dozen people or so I had been able to reach and invite to join the board. I didn't get any turndowns. Their names were important for advance release to the press.

The entire mass of material filled two suitcases which were heavy. Because I didn't want to make my entrance at the hotel, carrying them from the parking lot, I called Student Aid at the university and asked them to send someone over, telling them that the student would get a whole afternoon's work because he would have to stand by at a press conference I was attending and possibly run some errands for me.

13

Around one o'clock Miss Nettie called from down-stairs and said: "There's a Teddy Rodriguez here, Dr. Palmer. Says she's from Student Aid. Shall I send her up?"

"Says *she's* from Student Aid? Good God, I asked for a *he*."

"Well, it looks like a she to me."

It was a she, all right, nicely formed and very pretty, in faded denim hot pants, chopped-off short, blouse, and sandals. She looked vaguely familiar.

"Surprise, surprise!" she crowed. "I'll bet you expected a boy. But summertime, you know. You have to take what you can get. I just happened to be there."

"Teddy, do I know you?"

"I was in your English poetry class, Dr. Palmer. I'm the one who sat on the end, showing her beautiful legs and making eyes at you."

"Oh. Yes, of course."

"Aren't you thrilled?"

"Well, I would be, of course, except that I'm afraid you won't do. It's kind of a packhorse job and—"

By this time she was inside, pointing to the suitcases which were in the hall outside by bedroom door.

"Them? They're nothing." She skipped up the hall, grabbed them, and carried them to the alcove. "What's in them?" she said. "Bricks?"

"Pamphlets, press releases."

"I'm strong as a bull. Cheerleader during football season." She cartwheeled into the living room and then came back to me, walking on her hands. "See?" she chirped gaily, getting on her feet again. "Nothing to it."

"Then . . . you asked for this job."

"It's not the money—it's you."

"That's enough about me. Now, about lunch—"

"I had lunch. But I cook, too, as well as I do handsprings. If you want me to fix you some—"

"No, I had a late breakfast."

By then we were in the living room. She was looking at the pictures and I was wondering what to do with her, since the news conference didn't begin until four.

"O.K.," I said, "we're going to have some dead air, so sit down, make yourself at home, and help yourself to those magazines. *Time*, *Newsweek*, and *The New Yorker* are there on the cocktail table. While you're looking at them, I'll be boning up for the reporters."

She camped on one of the sofas with *Time* and I on the other sofa with the stuff Sam Dent's secretary had sent me, from a friend in the Newspaper Club, on the various local reporters who covered this kind of story. I thought it would help if I could call them by name, as though I knew all about them.

Pretty soon she pitched the magazine back on the table and said: "I know what we could do. I know what would freshen dead air."

"Yeah? Like what?"

She came over and sat in my lap and put her arms

118

around me. "Like we could go to bed."

"Like we could *not!*" I growled.

"We could, we could, we could!"

By that time she was kissing me—hot, wet, and sticky. Of course, Hortense completely possessed me by now, yet in just a few seconds I wanted this girl bad—and she knew it. There were more kisses; I don't know how many. But at last, by using all the will-power I had, I pushed her off, stood up, and said: "You wait downstairs—if you still want the job. Wait in the lobby. When I'm ready, I'll call Miss Nettie. Don't come up until she tells you."

"No, Dr. Palmer, no!"

"Yes. You have to go."

"But why? Dr. Palmer, I'm entitled! It's nothing new for me, that I thought it up after I got here. I fell for you right from the start, way back in September. I *showed* you my legs that first day when you lectured on Ann Rutledge."

"Ann *who?*"

"Whoever. Hathaway, I guess it was."

"Keep those Anns straight."

"And you peeped at my legs, too."

"So? They're pretty enough."

"And you want me *now.* I can tell!"

"Regardless of whether I want you or not, it can't be!"

"But why? Dr. Palmer, I ask you: *why?*"

"There's a reason, Teddy."

"Blonde or brunette?"

"More like blonde."

"I guess that says it."

She pulled out one of her curls, which were a sort of dyed sorrel, looked at it for a moment, and then shook

119

her head. Her eyes were wet. I felt compassion, deep and genuine. It seemed tragic, somehow, that I had to say no to her. I blotted her eyes with my handkerchief, while at the same time, edging her out. In the hall, when the elevator came, I kissed her once more and whispered: "O.K., I'll be thinking of you." When she was gone I went back inside, waited a minute, then called Miss Nettie and asked: "That girl from Student Aid—is she waiting or not?"

"She's sitting in the lobby."

I went into the bathroom and washed my mouth out with Listerine, to kill any smell of lipstick that might be lingering.

I sat down again, trembling. At three o'clock I picked up the suitcases and went down in the freight elevator to the parking lot entrance and carried them out to the car. After I had put them in the back, I went around to the front of the building into the lobby. There I found Teddy reading a magazine. She seemed upset that I had done my own toting.

"I wanted to do it for you," she said. "It's not the money. It's you."

"You said that already."

I put her in the car and for the first time noticed the patches on the seat of her pants. They looked as though some sailor had sewed them on.

"Who did your patches?"

"I did," she said. "Why?"

"Just wondering, that's all. They're nice, pattable patches."

"You ought to know. You patted them."

"So I did, so I did. Touchée."

"What do you mean, touchée? No one got touchéd,

120

I know of. Brother, what a washout. Patty cake, patty cake, pat me some more."

"What has to be, has to be."

When we reached the hotel parking lot I took the suitcases out for Teddy but let her carry them to the marquee where I told the doorman to take them and call a bellhop.

Conference Room A was just off the lobby. It was all set up, with the bar, buffet, and counter at one end, my service table at one side, three armchairs with their backs to the bar, mikes in front of them, and folding chairs facing them. We were the first to arrive except for a bartender polishing glasses and two girls in red trunks, boleros, and shoes, with some of the barest legs you ever saw. They were lining up bowls with dip, salad, and relish on the buffet, as well as placing platters of canapes around. They came running over to help. I introduced Teddy as "a working girl's working girl; so if you need any help, just holler." We all got along well. When the bellhop had taken the brochures and pamphlets out of the suitcases and left after getting his tip, Teddy and I arranged the material on the table. She had some suggestions about how to display it, all of them good.

14

Then the Garretts arrived. Hortense, wearing a green cocktail dress with a gold band around her head, looked simply beautiful. I presented Teddy as "my girl Friday who carried the press stuff for me so I could arrive like a *gran signor*—kind of like cruelty to children, except that she's as strong as a bull."

"How fortunate," Hortense said icily.

"But prettier'n a bull," Mr. Garrett said.

"Mrs. Garrett," Teddy cooed, "I've seen your picture often. I've always admired your hair. I just love dark blonde."

"You have quite beautiful hair yourself."

"Not really. Right now it's dyed with henna rinse. I wish it were blonde, like yours."

"I'll send you a wig. How's that?"

"Oh, Mrs. Garrett, *would* you?"

There was more to this exchange than met the naked ear. I was somewhat uneasy at the way Teddy was tipping me off that she knew what my reason was.

Hortense tried her chair and reached for the mike, to adjust it. But it was stiff and wouldn't budge. Teddy skipped over to it, and gave a yank that really did the trick. She pushed it a little bit at a time until Hortense nodded that it was the way she wanted it.

Hortense got up and came over to me. I was at the table I had had put in, looking at the various handouts. She nodded a couple of times. Then, after getting closer to me, she stiffened. "Get that girl out of here!" she snapped. "What do you mean, bringing such a creature?"

"*What* girl?"

"*That* girl!"

Her voice was pure venom, and she had the bad manners to point without looking where she was pointing, to the mikes where Teddy was standing. When she raised her voice, Teddy came over and took her wrist and began putting pressure on it. Hortense walked backward under the pressure of Teddy's grip until she reached her armchair and plopped down on it. When Teddy spoke, the mike, which was turned on, picked up her voice and boomed it out over the entire room.

"I saw what you did, Mrs. Garrett, leaning close in to Dr. Palmer, so you could sniff his shirt to see if it smelled like me. I'm sure it did. It should have, the way I climbed on him and twisted around in his lap and slobbered on him. But he said no. Did you hear what I said, Mrs. Garrett? He made me wait downstairs because he had a reason—kind of a *blonde* reason. All I can say is, if you're that reason, he might do better with me!"

She wheeled around and faced me, her eyes glittering with tears, and sobbed: "Dr. Palmer, I'll thank you to pay me, so I can go. I want my wages, whatever they are. Also taxi fare to the bus and bus fare to College Park."

But before I could get out my wallet, Mr. Garrett

124

came over. He wrapped Teddy in his arms and said very loudly: "Take it easy, Teddy. Calm down, relax. College Park is right on my way. As soon as we're through here, I'll run you home." He led her to one of the folding chairs, sat her down, and then went over to Hortense whose hand he picked up and patted, but she slapped him away. Then she jumped up and went out with that quick, boiling-hot walk a woman breaks into when she's really mad. She went through the lobby and out the front door.

I wasn't the first guy to get caught in the middle of by two women blowing their tops, but I felt like holy hell anyway. Mr. Garrett played it cool—adjusting the mikes, inspecting the food, conferring with the bartender, and joking with the girls. I sat on the table, watching him, trying to figure out where I stood, if anywhere. It was frightening, but I made myself own up to it, that here in just a few seconds, the whole ship had been blown out of the water. Mr. Garrett must know the truth now, whereas before he could only *guess*. How was he going to play it? And *was* he going to play it? But when he called me over, all he said was: "Lloyd, we'd better be getting ready." Which meant that he wasn't going to play it; he was just going to ignore it. I suppose for the moment it eased my mind, yet deep down inside, it left me more nervous than ever, because I didn't know *where* I stood. How *can* you ignore something like that? But if he could, I had to.

As I passed Teddy, I asked her: "Would you take charge of the press stuff? See that each reporter gets a release from every pile?"

"Okay, Dr. Palmer. I'm sorry."

125

"Why didn't you bring a stink bomb?"

"I said I was sorry."

"Don't bang at Teddy."

It was Mr. Garrett, who had come over to give her a pat. "We all make mistakes," he said, "especially when provoked."

That seemed to end the subject.

It didn't end Hortense, though. Pretty soon the reporters came, fifteen or twenty of them. Some I knew, at least by sight, and some I didn't, though on about half of them, I had done some background study. The two Washington papers sent men, and so did the *New York Times*, the *Los Angeles Times*, *St. Louis Post-Dispatch*, *Women's Wear*, and the Associated Press. But the *Wall Street Journal*, *Baltimore Sun*, and *Philadelphia Evening Bulletin* sent women, and for some reason, they took us over the jumps. The show got off to a lefthanded start when one of them pressed Mr. Garrett as to where Hortense was and why she wasn't there. "If the Institute is named for her, this show must be in her honor. What's become of her?"

But he didn't get excited. He answered: "She *was* here a moment ago, as a matter of fact; but then she changed her mind and left. My wife doesn't like cameras. They make her break out in a rash."

"Mr. Garrett," the woman said, "I know Mrs. Garrett quite well, and I've never noticed any allergy to cameras on her part. I would say she's not only photogenic but photogenerous."

"Then that's what you would say."

By this time three or four men were in front of us, sitting, standing, and kneeling, their cameras to their eyes, taking pictures of him. Instead of smiling,

126

though, all he did was look peeved. There are times when a stuck-out jaw is the one thing that wins the ball game, but a press conference isn't one of them. The woman smelled something peculiar about it, and she meant to get some answers. Suddenly she turned to me. "Mr. Palmer," she began.

"*Dr.* Palmer," Mr. Garrett corrected her.

"Dr. Palmer, in my paper's bio morgue I find eight envelopes on you, all in connection with football, but none that mentions biography. May I ask why you were picked to direct this institute?"

"Mr. Garrett picked me. Ask him."

"Mr. Garrett?"

"I picked him because he knows more about biography than anyone else," Mr. Garrett said. "He knows so much that it makes my head swim."

"Do you have a degree in biography?" she said to me.

"No, I haven't."

"Have you taken courses in biography?"

"There are no courses in biography."

"I beg your pardon?"

She was obviously caught by surprise. Some of the other reporters suddenly began writing furiously.

"There is no course in biography, or *discipline*, as they call it, in any American university that I know of," I said, "in spite of the fact that biography is the one literary field that Americans excel in. It was partly to fill this lacuna that I persuaded Mr. Garrett to endow the Hortense Garrett Insitute of Biography."

"*She* persuaded him, you mean."

"I know what I mean, if you don't mind."

"You've seen a lot of her, then?"

"Naturally. It was necessary in setting up

the Institute."

"At her apartment, we would assume?"

"If you would disconnect your assumer and stop telling me what I mean, we'd get along a lot better." That got a laugh, and I added: "I've never been to Mrs. Garrett's apartment. We've met for lunch and once or twice for dinner."

"How about your apartment?"

Well, how about my apartment? How much home-work had this woman done before today? Hortense was practically living at my apartment. Had she been seen even once coming or going from there?

I had to take a chance. "She has never been there."

"But *I* have!" Teddy chimed in.

"That's right," I said. "She's my weakness now."

"And mine, too," Mr. Garrett said.

"I'm Dr. Palmer's packhorse," she explained, "because I'm as strong as a bull. I also do back hand-springs."

She did a back handspring in the space between the folding chairs and the door. There was a stampede by those with cameras to get a shot of her doing it. But as she straightened up, she shied off.

"Hey, wait a minute," she called; "not so fast with them pop-ups. You take a picture of me, I must have my patches showing. It's my sorority rule. Okay, on my face, if you want it—but the patches have to be in."

"Darling," said the woman who had been badgering me, "one earthshaking gadget has not been invented yet—one permitting the camera to take your front end, where your face is positioned, and your hind end, where your patches are, at one and the same time. Do—"

128

"Aw? Then earth, stand by to get shook."

She turned to the table, moved piles of stuff to one side, then climbed on and did a hand stand, facing the cameras. But, of course, that put her shapely bottom just above her face.

"Okay," she said calmly, "shoot!"

They shot.

She hopped down, telling them: "That'll be fifty cents, please. Four bits from one and all."

Nobody moved to pay her. "Well, there's their trouble right there," she announced with an airy wave of her hand. "The media, I'm talking about. They're mean, they're chincy, they're cheap. Making cracks about a wife right in front of her husband, and on top of that, not paying the human packhorse who's posing for her picture. I do a handstand and what do I get? Nothing!"

"Teddy."

"Yes, Mr. Garrett?"

"Have a Kennedy half-dollar."

"You mean, shut up?"

"I'm too polite to say it."

"O.K."

She was quite meek about it. She pulled his face down and kissed him. They seemed to get on very well.

When Mr. Garrett had returned to his chair and Teddy was tucked away at the end of the table, the same woman reporter resumed with me.

"Dr. Palmer," she asked, "have you actually written a biography?"

"It so happens that I haven't."

"Aw!" Teddy yelped once more. "Dr. Palmer, why

don't you tell her? Why do you let her run over you?"
Then to the reporter: "You're damn right, he's written
a biography—William Shakespeare's! He wrote his
dissertation on Shakespeare for the Ph.D. he has. He
gave us a free copy—some of us, anyway—in his English poetry class, and it's wonderful to read! All about
the sonnets! And the Dark Woman; he *idemnifies* her!
It's like a detective story, only real."

That doesn't sound like much of a time bomb, but it
caused me more trouble than any other thing that happened that day. I had intentionally not mentioned
Shakespeare, because that's one thing you learn: Lay
off him. Don't bring up the subject unless, for some
reason like teaching a poetry class, you have to. Because you're just opening a can of worms. There's an
expert on every block who knows more about it than
God, all ready to show you up, and no matter how
sharp your research is or how silly the previous research, you'll get a drumming out of town that will
make the Lion and the Unicorn sound like a moment
of silence.

I ignored Teddy, but Mr. Garrett called her name.
When she answered, he said it this time: "Shut up."

"Yes sir."

"Who was the Dark Woman?" another reporter
asked.

"For that," I told him, "send three dollars and fifty
cents, plus postage, to the Lord Baltimore Press and
ask them to send you *Shakespeare and the Sonnets, A
New Look at an Old Subject*, by Lloyd Palmer.

"Who's the outstanding American biographer?"
asked one of the women reporters, at last bringing the
discussion back to the reason for our being there. And
on that, I decided to talk.

"The list is so long," I told her, "you'd be helpless to pick out one name. For my money, James Parton's *Life of Andrew Jackson* has had a greater effect on biographical writing than anything else I know of. He got away from the literary style of Prescott, Parkman, Sparks, and the other early writers and introduced the simple, easy, intimate, colloquial way of writing that later writers followed, such as H. H. Bancroft, Sandburg, Leech, Tuchman, *The New Yorker* "Profile" writers, and a host of others. You have to remember, when you're talking about American biographers, that the roster runs into the thousands. Then there are the wholesale biographers—Sparks with his *Library of American Biography*; Bancroft, with his *Chronicles of Builders*; Marquis with his *Who's Who in America*, and Sammons and Martindell who followed Marquis as publishers; and very importantly, Adolph Ochs, of the *New York Times*, who bore the expense of the *Dictionary of American Biography*, that prodigious trove of biographical information in twenty volumes. We should also honor Dumas Malone, the Jefferson scholar and dean of our biographers. But let us never overlook the *first* American biographer, Mason Lock Weems, whose preposterous *Life of George Washington*, the one with the cherry tree in it, went through seventy-one editions and is kept in print by the Belknap Press of Harvard University."

"He can talk all night if you have all night," Garrett said. "Personally, I've heard enough. Are we finished? Is there anything else you want to know?"

There didn't seem to be, so he signaled to the girls who began serving refreshments and cocktails. Then he called: "Come on, Teddy, we have to be running along."

"I want something to eat."

The girl with the tray of canapes wrapped some in a paper napkin and tucked them in Teddy's bag. But she still wouldn't go. She was rubbing her thumb with her finger at me, meaning *pay me*. Garrett said: "I'll take care of her, Lloyd." Then he smacked her on the patches, saying: "Get going!"

15

At last the nightmare of an afternoon came to an end and I was left alone with my pamphlets and a boy the head bellhop had lent me, who helped gather the stuff together, pack it into the suitcases, and carry it to the car. I drove to the Royal Arms where Irene gave me dinner, and then on home. I went in the front way to pick up any messages, but there hadn't been any. Then, when I opened the apartment door I caught the smell of perfume. I set the suitcases down, closed the door, and went to the living room. There in the dark, on one of the sofas, was Hortense, her eyes black and big as saucers.

"Well!" I said. "Hello. Didn't expect you so soon."

She jumped up, raced to the door, yanked it open, and peered out into the hall. "Where is she?" she snarled.

"Where is who?"

"That girl. That floozy."

"If you mean Teddy, your husband took her home—or at least, I hope he did. That's what he said he was going to do. She's a sweet girl who wants to get laid."

"And you laid her, didn't you?"

"So happens, I didn't."

"You expect me to believe that?"

"Yes, I do, and I'll prove it."

"You mean you'll make her tell me, and that will—"

"No, that's not what I mean."

I took hold of her, lifted her, and carried her into the bedroom. When I had dumped her on the bed, I started taking her clothes off. Her dress, the one she'd had on at the hotel, was no problem, but the panty-hose were. She kept fighting me off when I tried to peel them down. I'd spank her on the tail and in between make a grab for the pantyhose, and at last I had them off. Then I raped her, if you can call it that when you get full cooperation. When it was over I said: "Okay, that proves it, I think. Even a studhorse has only one of them in him per day. If Teddy had got it, I couldn't have given it to you."

She didn't answer. Then, after a moment, she asked: "Lloyd, what do we do now? That crazy girl spilled it."

"*You* spilled it, Hortense."

"I was furious. I could smell her on your clothes."

"And what you spilled can't be poured back in the bottle. As you've said so often, 'He may be many things, but he's not dumb.' "

"What did he say after I left?"

"He said, 'We'd better be getting ready.' "

"That was all?"

"Yeah, that was all."

We talked about it awhile, then the phone rang. It was Mr. Garrett. After asking if anything had happened after he left that he should know about and after I had said no, he said: "Lloyd, I finally persuaded Teddy that if you had a blonde reason for making her wait downstairs, that reason wasn't my wife. So that source of gossip is under control—or so I hope. But what I don't understand is why you brought her in the first place. My wife, I assume, is no vainer than the next woman. Just the same, women hate it when other women muscle in on their act, whether romance is involved or not, especially pretty ones like Teddy who do handstands for the cameras. Didn't you have any more sense?"

"Sir, I never gave it a thought, I wasn't guilty of anything with her, and since romance wasn't involved—"

"You mean with my wife?"

"Yes, of course that's what I mean."

He harangued me for another minute or two—about Hortense, about women in general, about using good judgment—but all I could think of was that at last I had lied to him—head on, direct. It always seemed that I couldn't have any more reason for feeling like a rat, but then it turned out that I could. He switched back to Teddy. "All I can say is, I envy you your willpower, giving her a brush—if you actually did. If it had been me, I'll freely admit, I would have been tempted."

"I was tempted."

"What a sweet kid."

"Yes, Mr. Garrett, she's all of that."

I had no sooner hung up than a wallop hit my cheek, and the hot venom poured in my ear. "So! *I was tempted*'! Then take that! And that! And that!"

The wallops kept coming, but I had had enough. I whipped the cover off and let her have it on her bare bottom. Of course she screamed bloody murder.

135

The next morning she was snoozing away in my arms when all of a sudden, she woke up and, leaning on one elbow, said: "Lloyd, when was my last period?"

"I haven't been keeping track."

"Neither have I."

"But aren't you on the pill?"

"Some kind of way, I guess. I hate it."

16

I almost jumped out of my skin around sunup at the sound of the phone ringing. When I answered, a man said: "Dr. Palmer? Dr. Lloyd Palmer?"

When I said it was, he said his name was Dennis or Henderson or Henson, or something like that, that he was doing a biography of John Adams, "one of my American patriot series, which, no doubt, you've heard of. They're school texts all over the country, standard for eighth, ninth, and tenth grades. And I wish you would put me down for a grant-in-aid from the Hortense Garrett Institute."

I suppose he said more before I could slow him down, put away the receiver, get up, go to the closet, get a pen from my coat, come back, and ask him to repeat what he had said. By this time, Hortense was awake, leaning up on one elbow and staring at me, baffled.

I started him up again and made some notes on what he said. I told him that his application would have my serious consideration, but before hanging up, I couldn't resist the temptation to tell him that if he really wanted a grant-in-aid, calling me at such an ungodly hour was a poor way to get it. He seemed surprised, even insulted.

"I assumed," he said, "that in a fairly run organization, things go on a first-come, first-served basis." By this time I was not only annoyed but curious, so I asked him how he had got my name in the first place.

"In the *Republican*. I'm looking at it as I sit here."

The *Republican*, it turned out, was the Springfield, Massachusetts *Republican*, and he had got my number from Information.

I climbed back in bed but had hardly got under the covers when the phone rang again. This time it was a woman doing a book on Mary Baker Glover Patterson Eddy. She lived in Newark, New Jersey. Again I made notes. When the phone rang for the third time, I just banged it down and didn't answer. Then I took the receiver off the hook.

We lay looking at each other. By that time, of course, sleep was out of the question. I dressed and went down to the lobby for the paper. What it contained was enough to curdle your blood. At the top of one of the inside sections was a four-column shot of Teddy doing her handstand, face to the camera and backside just above it, with both patches showing. The caption read: WHERE WAS MRS. GARRETT?

But the main story made sense. It was mostly about me and what I had said about American biography, with quotations from my brochure and flanking photos of me looking oily and Mrs. Garrett looking annoyed. Then I called Western Union. When I told the girl who answered who I was, she said: "Oh yes, Dr. Palmer, we have some messages for you—three telegrams and two night letters. Will you hold on a minute? I'll read them to you."

I yelped: "No, no, no! Don't read anything. They're

138

what I called about. Will you mark them and anything else that comes: Mail—Don't Phone!" When she had that straight, I hung up, left the receiver off again, and let Hortense make me some breakfast. Then I said: "I have to go to town—into the District. If this is how it's going to be by wire and phone, the mail will be twice as bad, and I have to do something about it, make some arrangement with the Post Office."

"What about *this* phone?"

"I'll call the phone company and ask them to take over."

Dialing once more a number which the operator gave me, I got the business office. Their suggestion was to have the number changed to an unlisted one. I asked how long that would take, and the woman said a couple of days. When I asked what to do in the meantime, she said: "Well, can't you leave the receiver off the hook?"

"That's what I'm doing now."

"Then you're doing the right thing. . . . Oh, I almost forgot. The charge for switching you over will be ten dollars on your next bill."

"I'd pay a hundred."

The main post office in the District of Columbia is on North Capitol Street. There I talked with a Mr. Stone in one of those rooms at the end of an endless corridor covered with green linoleum. He listened, then talked into a hushaphone thing that he cradled on one shoulder. Then he said: "I would say that your institute's main problem is that it lacks an address. We have boxes at various rates. I would think the seven-fifty size would be right for you. That's seven dollars and

139

fifty cents a quarter. Or, if you prefer, we can give you a pouch. But I think the box would be best."

"I'll take the box."

I paid him. He got up, took some keys from a rack, gave them to me, saying: "In a moment, I'll show you where it is." He sat drumming his fingers, apparently waiting for something. In a moment a messenger came in and dropped a half-dozen letters in front of him. He glanced at them and then gave them to me. "You're right," he said, "you have quite a crop already."

The letters were addressed to me, the Hortense Garrett Institute, the Hortense Garrett Foundation, Hortense Garrett, and some other variations. I picked them up and put them in my pocket, then went with Mr. Stone to a place on the first floor where there was an entire wall of boxes, all with numbers on them. He let me unlock mine. He asked if that would be all, and when I said it would and thanked him, he waved his hand and left.

I had taken care of wires, phone calls, and mail, but that was just the beginning. I had no more idea than the man in the moon what to do about the deluge of applications or, except in a general way, what the reason for it was. I had to have help, and I knew only one place to get it: headquarters. I went to the Garrett Building to phone Mr. Garrett in Wilmington. To my surprise, instead of being appalled at the turn things had taken, as I was, he was pleased, on the basis on what had come out in the Wilmington papers. The Associated Press, instead of playing it cute, had carried a straight story about the Institute, with an account of what I had said, quotations from the brochure, and a few formal words from Mr. Garrett. It hadn't occurred to him yet that it was this straight story that was causing the trouble. It was an open invitation to anyone who might be interested to put in for a lump of the sugar. When I pointed this out to him, he began to laugh and told me I'd better come see him. So, without waiting around (it wasn't yet twelve noon), I got in my car and drove up.

He sat there in his office and listened very closely. "It seems to me," he said, "we have to make up our minds what we're trying to do. Is it to discover new talent and then encourage it? Or reward talent already proven? Or what?"

"On talent," I said, "let's forget it. There's so much talent for biography in this country that encouraging new talent is like encouraging fish in the sea to swim."

"What, then?"

"We have to check on talent, that we take for granted. But the main thing is the project an author has in mind. Is it worth our support?"

"And who will decide that?"

"*I* will, I should think. But my problem is, I don't know where to start. As things now stand, I'm swamped, utterly snowed under."

"Let me give it a mull."

So he mulled. Then he said: "I think you need a staff."

"Of researchers?"

"Of investigators, would be more like it—gumshoes like those I have down there in Washington. Not guys who dig into books, but who dig into people. Who'll get on the tail of these writers, find out who they are, what they've done, what they're up to now—and report. Then you can make up your mind."

"The staff will add to our overhead."

"But not as much as trying to do everything yourself. And, while we're on the subject, what other help will you need once we're actually going?"

"Christ, we're rolling *now*."

"Yeah, yeah, yeah, but—"

"Secretaries, for one thing."

"We take that for granted. What else?"

"A librarian. I have one in mind—a Dr. Chin. He's Chinese."

"Okay, get him. What else?"

"Chief researcher and probably four assistants— one for each main period of our history, for each of our main wars—Revolutionary, Civil, First World, Second."

"That sounds fine. What else?"

"A genealogist. You may think that's funny, but it's something every biographer faces. For some reason, he's expected to give the family tree for any person he writes on; but it's special stuff and—"

"You have someone in mind?"

"A man named Davis, at the Library of Congress. He's due to retire soon, and—"

"Then he can be had?"

"I think he would jump in our lap."

"Okay, tell him, jump."

"One other thing: our building—"

". . . will be ready in a couple of months."

He had an odd look on his face. He went on: "Those canvas wraps you see in the front of the building are to cover certain special alterations, such as a black granite front with brass lettering. But not a word of this to my wife. I want it to be a surprise. If she gets curious about it, just say that the contractor can't be hurried.

142

The permit, especially for the *sign*, as they called it at the District building, was more trouble than the rest of the building put together."

Back in Washington and into the Garrett Building to start lining things up, especially to find a secretary for me. When I called Hortense about one, though, she knew exactly the right lady, who started the next morning. She was middle-aged, gray-haired, and spectacled. She wouldn't have been *my* choice, of course, but she turned out to be good at her job. She suggested two girls to help out with the typing, answering the inquiries that kept coming in, picking up our mail at the Post Office, and running errands. But I needed the investigators most of all and happened to think of a retired professor at the University of Maryland who, I suspected, could size up applicants just by the way they typed. His name was Carter. I called him, and he was immediately interested. He also had a friend, just retired from the University of Pennsylvania, whom he would like to work with him. So I called this man, a Dr. Johnson, and hired him, too, on Carter's say-so. The day after that, they checked in, and Sam Dent found them offices. By now I had an office; Miss Koehler, my secretary, had an office; the two Ph.D. "gumshoes" had an office between them; and my two extra girls had offices. I must say, Dent treated me well. God knows how he did it, but he managed somehow. I was indeed "rolling," with things well under control.

By Saturday night, with the new phone number in

service and the wires, mail, and occasional press inquiries answered, I could sit back and relax and let Hortense do me a steak, which she did. But she seemed oddly withdrawn. After awhile I asked: "What's the trouble? Have I done something?"

"Yes, I guess that's it."

"Like what?"

"I'll tell you, all in due time."

But it wasn't until we were tucked into bed and she was in my arms that she whispered: "Lloyd, I'm pregnant."

"Well! I *did* do something, didn't I?"

"I got the lab report yesterday. I didn't want to tell you until you were out from under some of the pressures that have been plaguing you."

"The rabbit died, huh?"

"They don't use a rabbit now. There's some other test that's more certain. *Positive*, it said."

"How do you stand on time?"

"On time? What do you mean 'on time'?"

"How far gone are you?"

"With the life we lead, it's pretty hard to tell. But two or three weeks seems about right. Maybe three. No more than four."

"Then there's plenty of time."

"For what?"

"Surgery, I would assume."

She lay still for a long time without saying anything. "I would have to think about that," she said finally.

"And in the meantime? What's permitted?"

For a moment, she drew a blank, then: "Oh *that*! Why, everything . . . not only permitted; it's required. He needs it—or she does, whichever—for . . . encouragement. Psychological normality. What you make me feel, he feels, too, of course—or she does."

"Then what are we waiting for?"

"You sweet goof."

The next day she didn't go into town. She sat around with me, first by the window, looking out, then by the fireplace where I had built a fire because the heat hadn't come on yet. Besides, it was chilly outside. And when she wasn't doing any of these, she would walk around the apartment. That night, again in my arms, she said: "I'm not going to have it done."

"The abortion? . . . Well, it's up to you."

"I was warned when I had my miscarriage that if I ever had an abortion, it could mean the end of me—not my life but my capacity to have children. And I want this child. Deep down in me, I've been wanting it, wanting to have one by you. That's what's made me so careless—with that damned pill. Now you know, I wasn't really careless. I just hated it, hated the purpose of it."

"Then that's that."

"It is, Lloyd. It has to be."

"How can they be so sure?"

"You mean the doctors? Of what it would do to me? Lloyd, nothing is really sure about a woman's internal works. They explained it to me, I guess—with pictures and diagrams and all sorts of warnings about having a natural birth and not letting them do a Caesarian. I suppose I understood it. Anyhow, it convinced me that once this happens to me, I have to go through, or else. But you want me to have it, don't you?"

"Have what? The child?"

145

"The abortion."

"Give me a minute to think what I mean." At the end of a very long minute I said: "I want you to talk to Mr. Garrett—about a divorce."

"That's just what I *don't* want to do."

"It's what you *have* to do."

"Lloyd, who says I have to?"

"God says so, Hortense. At the end of nine months, minus two, three, or four weeks, an eight ball will roll over us so big it'll mash us flat—unless by then you're divorced and we can be married honestly, as we are in all ways right now, except the one way that'll do our child some good."

"But why can't I wait? Why do I have to rush?"

"I've just told you. In nine months, minus—"

"But, Lloyd, we have a triangle here—you, me, and *him*. He's up to something, too! Why can't I wait him out? So he comes to me. So *he* brings the subject up."

"The subject of divorce?"

"Of course! What else?"

It had a deep, crafty sound, but to my mind wasn't deep and not in any way crafty. It was simply, I thought, putting her head in the sand, hoping that if she did nothing, things would turn out all right. Because I loved her, however, I pretended to buy it big, telling her: "O.K., then, so be it. At least we know this much—something goes on up there."

"Up where, Lloyd?"

"Wilmington. Hortense, he *knows*. He has to know. We know he knows. O.K., then, we take it from there. Why is he being so nice? What is he up to, anyhow?"

"That's it! That's what I mean, Lloyd!"

So, O.K., we wait him out. He has to break

146

cover eventually."

"You know what they say that about?"

"I'll bite. What?"

"Tigers."

17

So we were in business, and just to make it official, I named an "executive committee," three members of our board, to ratify my decisions and, of course, draw moderate salaries. I called Davis and got his acceptance—his enthusiastic acceptance, I might add. But in regard to him, one funny thing happened. By this time I was making weekly trips to see Mr. Garrett, and one day he said to me: "Davis was in—happened to be passing through and dropped in to pay his respects."

"Oh? Well, he's an old-time bureaucrat. They polish their apples . . . always. It's automatic with them. 'Corridor politicians,' they're known as."

"He's after your job, Lloyd."

"He's *what*?"

"Bucking for director."

"He *is* an old-time bureaucrat, isn't he? What did he say, if you don't mind my asking?"

"Nothing. I go by the look in his eye. But if I can see it, you can see it, and my reason for mentioning it is: don't be upset. Use him. Let him scheme his head off. Your job is safe, whatever he does."

"Well . . . thanks."

"He's an oily son of a bitch."

"With me, he acts like a brother."

"Don't trust brotherly love too much."

Davis was in his midfifties, above medium height, slim, well-conditioned, and gray, with a quick, eager smile, as though what you just said was the most profound thing he had ever heard. He had a way of taking off his glasses and studying you two-eyed with a stare much more intimate than a four-eyed stare would have been. Sam Dent fixed him up with an office, but he was underfoot all the time, dropping in on me with bright and cheerful news about how long he had been a fan of mine, from back in my college days to my days playing football.

But he happened to live in Riverdale, down the road from me, and when he dropped by the apartment one night without any advance notice, *that* was bad. Fortunately I was dressed, though Hortense was already in bed. So, thinking fast, I played it friendly, having Miss Nettie hold him and tell him I would be down. I bounced into the lobby, glad-handed him, and apologized for not asking him up, explaining that the apartment was "in a mess." He said he had an errand in College Park and had dropped by to ask me out for a drink. I thanked him, saying: "That's a great idea, but I have some things to do. Could I take a rain check on it?"

In a few minutes he left, but Hortense was all jittery when I got back upstairs. "Lloyd," she said, "I'm so scared, and I don't even know what of."

"Me too."

"What are you scared of, Lloyd?"

"That's it. I don't know."

Unfortunately, I *did* know, and so did she.

In bed one night not long after that, Hortense whispered: "Know what I did today? I hired a private detective."

"Oh God, that's all it needs."

"What are you Godding about?"

"Don't you realize that he's bound to find one of those bugs in his office, apartment, or wherever, and when he does, he'll know who put it there? Hortense, we're on the spot, and *you're* the one who said it: we've got a tiger by the tail. *You're* the one who said let's not go borrowing trouble—or whatever it was you said. And here now, you do the one thing that could louse us but good. Because, if I were in his place, the one thing that would really burn me up would be a gumshoe on my tail."

"Are you done?"

"You call that guy off!"

"I've already paid him, Lloyd. His *retainer*, he called it. A shocking amount of money."

"I don't care what you paid him. Call him off."

"No, I won't."

"Boy oh boy, this is all we need."

"I thought of all that, what you just said, what it would mean if Richard caught me. So the first thing I said was that though I wanted to find out what is going on, I wanted no bugs or things of that kind. And that detective just laughed at me. His name is Mr. Hayes and he was awfully nice. I picked him out of the yellow pages, something about his ad seemed honest and decent. His office is in Bladensburg. Lloyd, he said: 'Such stuff is for books or movies or television. We

151

never use it.' I asked him what he did use, and he said: 'There's no mystery about it. We just ask around in a natural way, so as not arouse suspicion, and in a case like this, we generally turn up what's wanted. Because when a man starts playing around—especially a prominent, wealthy man—the woman he's playing around with talks. All the king's horses and all the king's men can't keep her mouth shut. With her, it's a piece of news she wakes up with every day and goes to bed with every night. So we find out who she talks to and let that person spill it. There'll be no trouble about it—and no backwash.' Then I said I knew who it was, but that I felt I had to be sure before going further, and—"

"Hey, wait a minute! When did this happen? Who *is* is, Hortense? And how did you find out?"

"Don't you know who it is?"

"I haven't the faintest idea."

"It's that creature. That floozy. Teddy."

"You've got to be putting me on!"

"Why would I be? In God's name, Lloyd, I couldn't put anyone on, not about this, I couldn't. I'm in a desperate spot, as you might recall."

"What makes you think she's the one?"

"He's been seen with her, that's what. He takes her to lunch right in the Conrad Hilton. He's had her up there in Wilmington at the Du Pont for lunch, for dinner, for God knows what else. She has a mink coat worth at least five thousand dollars. She didn't get *that* by her own unaided efforts."

"Or maybe she did."

"Well, now you're making sense."

"He did like her, that I have to admit."

"And we know what *she* likes, absolutely."

"Hey, don't *you*?"

In just a few weeks we had granted aid to six writers, one of whom was John Garner, a well-known biographer. The others weren't so well known, though all had been published, and all were embarked on large-scale projects. Garner's project—Paul Revere—had an interesting angle. "I'll go into a riddle," he told me, "that no one has ever touched on so far, and yet it's there. He was a silversmith, everyone knows about that. But where did he get his silver? None was mined in the colonies, and any silver imported from Mexico, Peru, or wherever had to be paid for in gold. But there was no gold, and the lack of gold, together with Parliament's restrictions on paper money, for the benefit of English creditors, was one of the big causes of the American Revolution. If I can come up with an answer, I may make a contribution."

I gave him my blessing and he was appreciative, not only to me but to Davis as well, who was continually helpful to everyone, and to Carter and Johnson, my gumshoes, whose original report had O.K.'d him. I should have been excited about the prospects, and in a way I suppose I was, but with "modified rapture," as Koko put it. Because, while these various scholars had gone through the motions of thanking me, only Garner seemed to mean it. As a class, biographers turned out to be a monstrously churlish bunch. They acted as though they were doing us a favor by taking a hundred dollars a week. Once their thanks was given, they treated me like a lackey, Davis like dirt underfoot, and Carter and Johnson like subjects of a grand jury inquest. Davis would laugh at the look on my face, shake his head, and say to me: "Dr. Palmer, you haven't seen anything yet. Wait till you sign on with the Library of Congress, then get cornered by some busty bitch who wants to make Dame but so far only rates Daughter, and listen to her give out with what a bum you are for not being able to turn up the roster of Company B, Third New Jersey Riflemen for the year 1777. After that, which I put up with for twenty-two years, this bunch looks like a welcoming committee."

"But I've always liked and respected biographers."

"That's where the trouble starts—they like biographers, too."

"I guess you have a point."

18

I was pleasantly surprised at the invitation that came from the National Newspaper Club to address one of their luncheons and, of course, accepted. They were very cordial to me, inviting the Garretts, Davis, and Sam Dent at my request and giving me quite a build-up in their announcement. My talk was one I had given earlier to my classes at Maryland and other places, but this time I took extra care with it, especially the first part, the survey of American biography, which I tried to make short but not too short while at the same time keeping it interesting. Comparing it with the English and occasionally the German and French, I waved the flag a little, explaining in some detail how, and not only how but why, American biography leads the world. I touched on the English libel laws, "which are so silly that only in unusual cases does a writer dare choose as a subject someone livng or only recently dead." I went on to criticize the English version of *Who's Who*, "which only occasionally names the subject's mother and never names his children. In *Who's Who in America*, since the time of Wheeler Sammons, all the subject's children are named; but in the English *Who's Who*, one son and two daughters are considered enough to cover the subject. Well, that's a big help, isn't it, to the scholar who wants exact information?" That got a laugh, and I went on to our Institute, exploring the idea of it and demanding a hand for "our guide, friend, and generous backer, Mr. Richard Garrett." It really crackled out, and he seemed moved as he took a bow. Then I demanded another "for the gracious, understanding, and beautiful little lady whose name our Institute bears and who had labored so indefatigably with us to bring it into being, and who is with us today—Mrs. Hortense Garrett!" For her, they made it a standing ovation. She got up, blew kisses, and started to cry, so Mr. Garrett got his handkerchief out, wiped the tears away, and let her blow her nose. The little toot she gave was the biggest laugh of the day, and, of course, got a big hand. I couldn't top it, so I thanked them and sat down.

According to the Club's tradition, there is a question period following an address. Byron Nash, the president, was ready with several that had come up in writing while I was talking. I fielded them fairly well, occasionally getting a laugh—like the one on subjects I thought were being neglected, which biographers should give their attention to.

"It's not the Institute's policy to coach its writers," I said, "or to press ideas on them; but of course there are curious gaps in our literature that fairly cry out to be filled. For example, who was Mason? Or Dixon? They ran the most celebrated survey of all time, yet I find no more than a few lines about them in any reference work. Then there's Sally Benson who died just a few months ago. She was good-looking, gifted, and well known, but if you can find one word about her in any reference book, you have better eyes than I do. Then, of course, there's Bill Bailey—a real person, don't forget. I would call his fine-tooth comb the great mystery of all time."

That got a friendly laugh. I was about to sit down, but Mr. Nash stopped me with another question. Searching the room with his eyes and addressing a man in one corner, he said: "Jack Albaugh, as a mystery, your handwriting makes Bailey's comb seem like nothing. Suppose you step up and ask this question yourself?"

Albaugh stood up and came to the podium. There was something cocky about him, and I could feel an expectant stir in the room. He was small, gray-haired, and dapper, and he bowed to the applause before facing me.

"Dr. Palmer, at a press conference some time back, you claimed to have identified the Dark Woman in Shakespeare's sonnets. But you refused to go any further with your analysis, to say whom you were talking about. May I ask you to name her now, if indeed you can?"

I knew I was in for it. "I made no such claim," I said. "A girl in my employ at the time made it for me, quoting a book of mine, a doctoral dissertation and causing quite a stir. The press devoted more space to her backside, as well as the patches on it, than to our Institute. Of course, she did have a pretty backside which photographed well, but—"

In other words, I was trying to sidestep the question. Albaugh let me finish and then insisted: "I asked you to name the Dark Woman."

For a moment I paused. Then I said: "I think she was Ann Hathaway."

"The *wife*?"

"That's right."

He was astonished, and there were gasps from all over the room, because, of course, in the group were many who knew the sonnets and a few who had studied them. In a moment he went on: "May I ask you your grounds for this remarkable pronouncement?"

"It's not a pronouncement; it's one man's opinion. But since no one knows who this woman was, one man's opinion is as good as another's. I didn't start out to identify her. It fell into my lap as a corollary to some other things I stumbled on, other aspects of the sonnets. I started out with them as a doctoral assignment, one I picked with university approval. Then I began reading them carefully, over and over, for sense and anything else I could detect. Soon something struck me as odd: the first few, perhaps the first dozen, touch on a curious theme: should the writer play with himself or find himself a playmate? But this, I suddenly realized, is not something a grown man worries about, least of all *this* grown man who, don't forget, fathered a child at the age of eighteen. The next thing I noticed was that all of these early sonnets were obviously addressed to Shakespeare himself. Well, if some, why not all? At what point is this mysterious 'Mr. W.H.'— the object of Thorpe's dedication as the 'true author of these sonnets'—supposed to have entered the picture? I couldn't find any such point. To my ear, the writer was talking to himself all the way through, and 'Mr. W.H.' could well have been *Will Himself*—to make a stab at naming him. The next thing I noticed was the paucity of the background in the sonnets. The richness of *Macbeth, Hamlet, Lear,* and *Julius Caesar* is simply not in them. I counted the classical allusions and found exactly seven: one to Dian, as he calls her, and one each to Mars, Venus, Adonis, Cupid, Saturn, and Philomel. But seven allusions to classical figures, out of 2,166 lines of poetry, isn't very much. I was forced to the conclusion that these magical things were the work of a youth, an adolescent caught up in a narcissism that was hipped on his own beauty, with the vast reading of his adult years still to come and his delight in his own virtuosity just beginning to unfold.

Shall I compare thee to a summer's day?
Thou art more lovely and more temperate:
Rough winds do shake the darling buds of May,
And summer's lease hath all too short a date:
Sometimes too hot the eye of heaven shines,
And often is his gold complexion dimm'd;
And every hair from fair sometime declines,
By chance or nature's changing course untrimm'd;
But thy eternal summer shall not fade,
Nor lose possession of that fair thou owest;
Nor shall Death brag thou wander'st in his shade,
When in eternal lines to time thou grow'st:
   So long as men can breathe, or eyes can see
   So long lives this, and this gives life to thee.

"When I got that far with it, there was a simple deduction. In Sonnet 104 we get a fix on time, on how long these sonnets have taken:

To me, fair friend, you never can be old,
For as you were when first your eye I eyed,
Such seems your beauty still. Three winters cold
Have from the forests shook three summers' pride,
Three beauteous springs to yellow autumn turn'd

In process of the seasons have I seen,
Three April perfumes in three hot Junes burn'd,
Since first I saw you fresh, which yet are green.

"If we assumed that that curious phrase, 'when first your eye I eyed,' meant an eye eyeing an eye in a mirror and that this memorable moment when he first saw his own beauty came when he was fourteen, then he would now be seventeen, with a great event due in his life. At the age of eighteen he would court a woman, presently get her with child, and marry her. Sure enough, in Sonnet 127 we get it:

In the old age black was not counted fair,
Or if it were, it bore not beauty's name;
But now is black beauty's successive heir,
And beauty slander'd with a bastard shame:
For since each hand hath put on nature's power,
Fairing the foul with art's false borrow'd face,
Sweet beauty hath no name, no holy bower,
But is profaned, if not lives in disgrace.
Therefore my mistress' eyes are raven black,
Her eyes so suited, and they mourners seem
At such who, not born fair, no beauty lack,
Slandering creation with a false esteem:
    Yet so they mourn, becoming of their woe,
    That every tongue says beauty should look so.

"And so," I wound up, "for my money, Ann Hathaway was the girl—and there's another check on it: in Sonnet 129, two numbers past the one I just quoted, is voiced bitter disappointment in 'lust,' as he calls it, but disappointment that has meaning only if we assume that it's the disappointment of first flight—sex wasn't quite what he thought it would be—and once more we come back to Ann. There's another point to be borne in mind. 'Venus and Adonis' was published in 1593 when Shakespeare was twenty-nine, but perhaps it was written before that. It's about a woman in her twenties who is satiated with sex, is hungry for a new experience, and who falls for a boy in his teens. Ann Hathaway was twenty-six when she fell for Shakespeare, so this poem could well be a memoir of personal experience. The fact that no sonnet mentions the marriage might be explained by the gory finish that befell Adonis. The poem proves nothing, yet it is in harmony with the theory that 'Venus and Adonis,' far from being a fresh effort, was actually a continuation of these sonnets in another poetical form."

I stopped, and a murmur of incredulity went through the room. Albaugh, as though addressing a not-so-bright child, said: "Dr. Palmer, surely you're not serious in contending that these deathless poems are the work of a youth. At that time, a butcher's apprentice. And—"

"Mr. Albaugh," I said, "there's not one shred of real evidence that Shakespeare was ever a butcher's apprentice. It is assumed that he was on the basis of local heresay, as it was assumed that Mary Fitton was the Dark Woman until a window was found, one made in her honor, that proved she was a blonde. In my theory, I must confess, the precocity involved has bothered me, until a couple of years ago when the Maryland Arts Council sponsored a literary competition for high school students in the state and made me one of the judges. The compositions included poetry, even some sonnets, which astonished me. The best of them weren't just pretty good; they were damned good—fit to be published, of true professional grade. Poetry,

161

like music, is an art that blossoms young. If Maryland kids can write it, couldn't Shakespeake have? Let me quote a statistic: in *Bartlett's Familiar Quotations*, the King James Bible gets twenty-eight pages; John Milton, fourteen; John Dryden, seven; Longfellow, six; Edgar Allan Poe, three; and Tennyson, eleven. But William Shakespeare gets *seventy-seven*. It gives you some idea how great this genius was. Remember, all the others I mentioned were celebrities in their teens. Poe, for example, got out a published volume of verse before he was twenty, and Longfellow paid part of his Harvard expenses by writing verse for the papers. I say, for God's sake, let's stop thinking of this man as just an average boy, a glover's son from Stratford who went down to London for some reason, held horses in front of the Globe Theatre, got stagestruck inhaling the effluvia of grease paint, and then started writing plays, with sonnets in between. Genius isn't acquired, like a case of rickets. It's born. If Shakespeare was a genius at thirty-five, he'd have been a genius all his life."

"But Dr. Palmer, after all, fourteen—!"

"Mr. Albaugh," I shot back, "I've been waiting for you to say it—I staked you out. It just so happens that America's outstanding poet, at least most successful poet, was a success in life, a local Detroit celebrity, on the basis of paid contributions of poetry to the *Free Press* at fourteen. I ask you, if Edgar A. Guest could do it, couldn't William Shakespeare?"

It caught them by surprise and got a tremendous roar, first laughter and then hand-clapping. With that, I stalked back to my table. When I bowed and sat down, Hortense patted my hand. Sam Dent

162

thumped me on the back, and I had to stand up again as the applause kept on.

That night she phoned to say she would be late. "Richard has something he wants to show me. He's asked me to dinner first." So I undressed, put on my pajamas and a robe, and waited. I waited for a long time. It wasn't until after eleven that the elevator stopped at my floor and I heard her putting her key in the lock. After kissing me, she said: "Darling, I have to ask you to get dressed and come out with me. There's something I have to show you, something Richard took me to see so I could see it first with him. But, of course, I want to see it with *you*."

"What is it?"

"He surprised me with it, and I want to surprise you."

So she helped me dress, and we went downstairs to her car, which she insisted we take because she wanted to drive. She followed Rhode Island Avenue in as far as Sixteenth, where she turned and entered an all-night parking garage. As soon as she had her ticket she took me by the hand and led me down to K Street. She turned into it, and then suddenly we were standing across the street from our building, the new one I had had Garrett buy. But I hardly recognized it. All the scaffolding, canvas, and boards were gone, so that the front was clear, with its new black granite facing covering the entire front. And there in big bright, brass letters was:

THE
HORTENSE GARRETT INSTITUTE
OF BIOGRAPHY

• • •

It was lit by soft golden floodlamps, and a shiver went through me.

"Isn't it beautiful?" she said softly.

"I have to say it is."

"I love to look at it. I wanted to . . . with you."

"You're consecrated to fame."

"It's not that. It's just that—it's so *beautiful!*"

"It is, it certainly is. The lettering is art in itself, and that stone—its color and the way it's polished—is simply staggering."

"It comes from Minnesota. They polish it out there and then ship it in slabs by flatcar, all cut to size and ready to install. Richard had to pay all kinds of bonuses to get it done so quick, but, of course, he has a magic wand."

"Where's that light coming from?"

"From the building behind us, the one across the street. More of the magic wand; but when it waves *for* you, it's something."

"Something to see—it certainly is."

"Well, you might show some enthusiasm—a little, anyway."

"I *have* shown enthusiasm. You want me to jump up and down?"

"That's what I want to do."

"Then—"

I started jumping up and down, but she stopped me in horror after glancing around to see whether any police were there. Then, very sulky, she said: "You looked like a fish flopping—and that's how cold you are."

"O.K., but what did I have to do with it?"

164

"It was your idea, Lloyd."

"It was *his* magic wand."

"And I helped a little, didn't I?"

"Hortense, without you, it wouldn't have happened."

"You really mean that?"

"I do. At least we know I love you."

"I opened my mouth to say, 'Then act like it,' but the trouble is, you might—right here on K Street."

"I'd be tempted, I certainly would be."

"Let's go home. . . . But first, let's walk up to the Hilton and see what the paper says about the brawl you got into this afternoon. Then we can come back for one last look."

At the Hilton, which was just a block away, the stack of papers was out front on the sidewalk. The rope was being cut off as we got there, and when they were brought inside, we bought two. Then we sat down with them in the lobby. I was covered in the section devoted to goings-on around town, in two separate stories, one devoted to what I had said about biography and the other to my verbal brawl with Albaugh on the subject of Shakespeare. It was that one that gave me concern. Instead of kissing me off as someone in over his depth, however, the article was respectful. The reporter knew his Shakespeare. For the benefit of those who didn't he explained the sonnets a bit, especially the mystery of "Mr. W.H." and the Dark Woman and went on to report word for word what I had said. At the end he commented: "It is a novel theory, and it has one point to commend it: it rests on the incontrovertible fact, as he insisted to his listeners, that his was the greatest genius in the history of language—ours or any other."

"Well," Hortense said, "aren't you pleased?"

"Yeah, I guess so."

"*I* am. I'm proud of you."

"Okay, I love to be prouded of."

"I want to go home now."

"Then let's go."

"But let's look one more time."

We looked at the building once more and then got in her car and started home. She made me drive. "I'm too proud to drive," she said; "my mind wouldn't be on it."

We were just falling asleep when it popped into my mind to ask: "Any word from your gumshoe?"

"Now why do you bring that up? Why, on this night of nights, do you have to ask that?"

"You're five months gone, that's why."

"And why do you have to say *that*?"

"Because it's true."

She cracked up, crying and refusing to let me touch her. In every way, she made a production of it. Then at last, she said: "She hasn't started yet. The one Mr. Hayes wants to put on it is Finnish but speaks Swedish, too. He thinks she could start by asking Inga for a job and then when Inga says no, to sit down for a minute or two to pass the time of day. It seems she's good at that kind of thing, and Mr. Hayes thinks Inga could be of considerable help. The housekeeper always knows, he says, what the master is up to, and she might pass out stuff to a visitor she liked. The girl, Mr. Hayes says, has made an art of sociability."

"Sociability helps."

"Does that answer your question?"

"It's what I wanted to know."

"Kiss me." And then: "Lloyd, I'm getting terribly nervous."

19

Of course, once we moved into the building, Hortense wouldn't have been Hortense without giving a party, a big stinkaroo in celebration thereof, although she called it an "opening" and acted as though it was something anyone would do under the circumstances, or, as she put it, "the least we can do, in all decency." But I was beginning to find out that all she knew to do or that rich people like her knew to do about anything—from the birth of an heir to the shotgun wedding preceding it—was a little party for three hundred people or so. What such parties accomplish I haven't yet found out except to make Hortense take a deep breath and say, "Thank God *that's* over"—and then begin planning the next one.

But if it would make her happy—and, especially, ease her mind—it was all right with me, and I pitched in to help to the extent that I could. My help consisted mainly of moving the Institute in so we would have something to celebrate. It was quite a job, and I called on secretaries, Dr. Lin, our Chinese librarian, Carter and Johnson, and, of course, Davis. Our quarters took up three floors of the new building, including the first floor. There, through a heavy glass door was the big room I've already mentioned, now finished in oak paneling and furnished with bookshelves, desks, leather chairs, and thick carpeting. It was to be our reception room, with secretary, phone, and the usual intercom hookup. Beyond was my private office and beyond that, Hortense's and beyond that, a small dining room with bar, kitchen, and pantry. Her mind, though she apparently didn't realize it, ran to the entertainment and facilities it required more than to the conference rooms upstairs.

But not Davis's mind. He had ideas about our library. The minute he started to talk, I knew they were good. His point was that fifty percent of our subjects would figure in one of America's wars but that a lot of references to them would be found in standard works which weren't too expensive to buy—for example, for the Civil War, the Official Record; for Battles and Leaders, the Southern Historical Society Papers, the Photographic History, and the Bassler collection on Lincoln. He thought if we stocked these books, it would save all kinds of work for our scholars, and they wouldn't have to go to the Library of Congress or the National Archives or wherever, but would have them right at hand there in our own building. I agreed and authorized him to buy sets wherever he could. All that summer he had been making his deals, which was how he came to have all those books in storage. They had to be moved in now by truck and then hauled up to the second floor and shelved. In front of the shelves we put rolling ladders, index cabinets, and desks. I copied the room from what I had heard of a scholar's room—Rupert Hughes—in Los Angeles, which was a model of efficiency, I had heard. On the third floor were the "study rooms" for our "fellows." The other seven floors we rented out, and this led to a small brouhaha just before the big bash. Donald Klein, our rental agent, had his desk inside the front door where he took it for granted that he could buttonhole guests as they came in regard to rental space. Of course Hortense hit the roof when I told her and went boiling downstairs to see him. I went along, unhappily, not believing in brawls and hoping she wouldn't start one. But count on her: "Don," she said, "of all the people I wanted to come, I think I wanted you the most, and here I find out you're going to sit at this desk and *sell*! Don, how could you? Oh, how could you!?"

It turned out that he couldn't.

There was no particular reason for me to be nervous that day. Hortense had lined everything up down to the last detail, especially my part in it. But for some reason, I *was*—plenty. As director, I was to stand with her and Mr. Garrett and help receive the guests, dividing with Sam Dent the job of supplying names, though since he had no official connection with the Institute, he didn't stand in the receiving line. But because he knew the Garrett staff and, of course, the politicians, and I knew the fellows, board members, scholars, and Institute staff, it seemed that between us, we had everyone covered. It was my first big Washington party, however, and I had a lot to learn.

I felt something, something more than I had expected, the moment I get there around four, with things due to start around five. It may have been the baby grand piano that had been moved in without my knowing it or the bull fiddle in its case, leaning in one corner. Or it may have been the chrysanthemums, the big jardiniers full of yellow ones, standing in all four corners and in rows against the wall. Or it may have been the half-dozen black girls in the dining room whom I glimpsed through the open doors—the caterer's contingent, in dresses so short there was probably a law against them—bare legs, bare midriffs, skimpy bras, and little lace caps and aprons. Or it may have been the black girl at the desk, dressed the same way, who was reading a magazine and who put her hand on the phone when I went over to call Hortense, saying: "Sir, this phone is for incoming calls only. I can't let you use it. There's a pay phone in the lobby." Or it may have been Hortense's manner when I went out in the hall and called her—the quick brush she gave me, as if to say she was busy and would I kindly leave her alone. Whatever it was, I finally got it through my head that something was about to happen. And, of course, I tried to get with it, which is a bit hard to do when you have no idea what you're trying to get with.

Sam Dent arrived, and I asked him what was up, but he gave me a vague answer: "If I knew, I'd certainly tell you; but nobody does, actually. They think they do, but they can't be sure."

The Garretts arrived and Hortense gave me a quick briefing: "You'll stand with us, receive the guests first, and present them. Sam will present them to you and you will present them to us. For heaven's sake, listen for names and get them straight. Repeat them clearly to *us*." She took her place with Mr. Garrett, at the upper end of the room near the door of my office, and I took mine with them; she was standing next to me, with Mr. Garrett on her right. The orchestra came in and began to tune up. The bass player took his fiddle

172

out of the case.

The guests began to arrive and were met by Sam who herded them to the front of the room toward the windows. If was barely five o'clock, yet dozens of people were there, some looking out at the street as though expecting something. Everyone seemed to know what was coming off except me, and I began to feel queer. The orchestra struck up with "Ma, He's Making Eyes at Me."

The phone rang, the one for incoming calls, which the girl had refused to let me use. She answered it and then signaled to Mr. Garrett who was there in three strides. He answered, nodded, and handed the receiver back to the girl. Then he nodded to Hortense and they went out in the hall and from there to the sidewalk. Finally I knew what it was: the call was from the White House to say that the President's car had just left. That's what all the excitement was about.

By now everyone was at the windows, watching, and I watched, too, from the doorway. A car pulled up and six men got out, like in a gangster movie, four of them staying outside, two-and-two, to block the sidewalk, and the other two coming inside to stand around gimlet-eyed, studying the crowd. Then another car pulled up, a limousine with the blue-and-white Presidential seal on the door. Then the President was getting out and holding his hand for the First Lady. Then they were coming in with Mr. Garrett and Hortense. The orchestra leader, who by now was standing beside me, made a sign and the orchestra broke off what they had been playing and rolled into "Hail to the Chief." The President waved to them and took his place with the Garretts where they had been before, up near the door of my office, the First Lady

173

beside the President and the Garretts beside her. Hortense beckoned to me and I went over. When I was presented, the President said: "Dr. Palmer, it's a pleasure I've looked forward to. I've seen you play often."

"He's a fan of yours, Dr. Palmer," the First Lady said.

From there on in, it went smoothly. Sam formed the guests into line and brought them to me, and I latched onto the names, which wasn't hard, since they were all prominent people—senators, cabinet officers, congressmen, judges, writers, scholars, librarians, and so on. It was quite a distinguished gathering. Senator Hood was there with Mrs. Hood, but they seemed somewhat subdued.

The orchestra resumed its lively tunes, and when everyone had been received, the President stood around, chatting affably. I made a point of not staring. Then I felt a hand on my arm, and when I turned, he was standing beside me.

"Dr. Palmer, I saw you do something once that baffled me, and I've promised myself that if I ever met you, I would remind you of it and ask you to clear it up."

"Sir, if I can, I'll be glad to."

"It was in a game with Virginia. In the last quarter, one of Virginia's players scooped up a Maryland fumble and headed for a touchdown, with you in hot pursuit. Now, I had noticed your clean tackling—you left your feet, hit them clean, and brought them down hard. But when you closed in on this man, you didn't tackle him the way you usually did. You went up his back, threw an arm around his neck, and wrestled him to the ground with about as much style as a fireman throwing a mattress out the window. I knew there had to be a reason. . . . So what was it? Do you remember the play?"

"I remember it—the game, the play, the tackle. It was cold that day. There were snow flurries, and our hands were so numb that we couldn't handle the ball. Both teams kept fumbling, and passing was out of the question. To tackle a man from behind, you had to grab what you could and hold on—pants, padding—anything. You couldn't knock a man down by impact; there wouldn't be any. He would be running the same way you were and just about as fast. But what could I do that day? My hands were so cold I couldn't hold on, so I had to clip him and take the penalty or else go up his back. I hated it; it's such a crummy way to play. But I did it. I brought him down, and we won the game. Does that clear it up?"

The President nodded, apparently in admiration. Then he smiled.

"It never occurred to me," he said, "what the reason was, but I knew there had to be one. I always admire someone who does what has to be done—when, as Grover Cleveland put it, he 'faces a condition, not a theory.' "

He turned to someone else then, and my other arm was caught, this time by Hortense.

"I heard it," she whispered. "Aren't you proud?"

"I guess so, but why couldn't you have told me who was going to be here?"

"Oh, I couldn't! We weren't sure he would be. Even after he accepted, something could have come up. He would have been represented, of course, but that would have been awful—to let it out that he was going to be here and then have him not come. *And*, the Secret Service asks you not to make an announcement. If it's not known, the danger is that much less."

"Everyone knew but me, apparently."

That night she paraded naked in front of the full-length mirror, asking me: "Lloyd, does it show on me? I *am* five months gone, as you said, and tonight that Judy Hood looked at me rather peculiarly. She had a certain look in her eye."

"Turn around. Slowly."

She turned, and I said: "Nothing so far."

"It won't be long now, and I still haven't heard from that Finn."

"Not to hurry you—"

"I know, I know, I know."

20

That day marked the zenith of Lloyd Palmer's star as director of the Hortense Garrett Institute. After that, it began to fall—or, I could even say, plunge. That same week we took on more writers, more biographers, with study rooms, recorders, secretaries assigned to transcribe, and all the rest—including a man I won't name. He was from Georgia and was doing a book on Longstreet, who was briefly Lee's second in command. That doesn't sound like anything trouble could grow out of, but what that biography did to me shouldn't happen to any American citizen who pays taxes and obeys the law. This writer was well known. He was the author of a fine book on Francis Marion, the Swamp Fox of Revolutionary fame, as well as many historical articles in important publications. In other words, he seemed worthy in every way of the grant-in-aid we gave him, in addition to office accommodations.

The first indication that there might be something odd about him was when Davis dropped by my office and suggested that "you leave him to me," a hint I disregarded because I was beginning to distrust all hints from Davis. So when this man came in, I asked him to lunch. I took him to Harvey's and listened while he talked—or at least, half-listened, for he began to bore me early on. I dislike people with grievances. His was against Douglas Southall Freeman, the biographer of Lee and Washington—and, it seemed, of Longstreet as well. That, this man could not forgive Freeman for.

"So, okay," he growled, "we know about Gettysburg, how Longstreet wanted to shift his corps to the right and hit the Union rear and cut them off from their road, and perhaps, with luck, roll them up for a surrender. And we know that Lee said no and insisted on Pickett's charge, one of the worst decisions yet made on a battlefield. So, okay, that was it; that was how Freeman had to tell it so long as the subject was Lee. But couldn't he leave it at that? Did he *have* to write Longstreet up year after year for every newspaper, quarterly, and publisher who wanted a piece on the subject? Couldn't he have disqualified himself? Because he must have known, Dr. Palmer, that to make a star out of Lee, he had to make a bum out of Longstreet! But Longstreet was right that day at Gettysburg! He was not a bum! And I say Dr. Freeman was wrong to keep on defaming him! He shouldn't have! He did not have the right! Why did he have to be Longstreet's biographer, too?"

He was getting so worked up that the maitre d' began shooting looks at us, and I tried to quiet him down. "Hold it," I said, "I agree that Freeman might well have stepped aside and let someone else write on Longstreet, but, after all, Longstreet is dead and Lee is dead and Freeman is dead. It's your turn now, but bury the dead, why won't you?"

"You have no objection, then?"

"What objection could I have?"

178

"You're furnishing me with money, which could give you the idea that you control what I say. Well, get this, Dr. Palmer, *I* control what I write. *I* do, not you! Sir, did you hear what I said?"

"Hey, hey, hey."

He shut up and I told him: "The Hortense Garrett Institute passes no judgment on what you write, nor does the Institute try to control it in any way. All we ask in return for our help is a book."

"Then you accept my way of doing it?"

"I accept your writing your own book."

That's how things stood until he was invited to address a convention of the United Daughters of the Confederacy in Atlanta. There he not only shot off his mouth about his book but repeated his remarks about Lee and what Freeman had done to Longstreet, one of Georgia's eminent sons. Then he dragged me into it, claiming that I had accepted his "whole idea" as proof of the gains he was making "in swaying scholarly opinion, so justice can be done at long last to a great man's reputation." He spoke along these lines for an hour, with photographers taking his picture, reporters taking notes, and ladies taking exception. Because some were fans of Robert E. Lee and one or two were fans of Freeman, there was an argument, which was fine with the newspapers, and not just those in Atlanta, but papers that subscribed to the Associated Press. The story appeared in Washington and Wilmington.

Mr. Garrett called, wanting to know what was up. When I told him, he said: "We're in for it, then. Sam Dent just reported. We're to be peeled tomorrow, have our shirts ripped off by old blabbermouth himself, Senator Pickens of Georgia, who's going to let us have it on the floor of the Senate. He'll wave the Confederate flag. What else he'll wave, we don't know, but I wouldn't put anything past him. He's up for re-election this year, and to have this drop in his lap—a chance to defend God, the Confederacy, *and* Robert E. Lee all in one fell swoop, while being racist and yet pretend he's not—that's something he could have prayed for but never believed could happen. So keep your head down. It could be bad."

Sam Dent was in and out all day, but around five he came in and sat down, looking sullen. "That stupid son of a bitch," he growled, "we pay him a hundred a week, give him a girl, room, phone, and free phone calls, and this is his way of showing his gratitude. And it's a mess, Lloyd. That rotten Pickens is milking it. He's going to give us the works."

"All right—but *what* works?"

"Hearings . . . before his subcommittee."

That meant the Subcommittee on Internal Revenue, or whatever its title was, of the Senate Finance Committee, which Pickens was chairman of. They had been looking into tax-exempt foundations, some of which had unquestionably been getting away with murder. So far, they hadn't bothered us, but legally we were under their jurisdiction. I said: "I guess we're in for it, then."

"I would say *you* are."

"Me? Personally?"

"I hate to upset you—but yes, you are."

"How? In what way? What have I done?"

"I don't really know, Lloyd, but if there's one worst way you can think of, that's the way it's going to be.

This guy is a rat."

I could think of a way.

And from the way Sam looked at me, so could he.

The hearing was held in Room 2227 of the Senate Office Building, which is the Finance Committee's room. Since it met on Wednesday, our hearing was scheduled for Monday of the following week. I received a subpoena to testify, which was served by a man who seemed not to have any face. He touched my coat with it, dropped it on my desk, and left without saying a word. Mr. Garrett also got an invitation, delivered the same way by the same man. By this time he had come down from Wilmington and checked in at the Hilton, "so you won't be bothered by endless phone calls," he told Hortense. "Actually," she explained to me, "so I can stay with you without his seeming to know. He's so sweet."

"*If* you stay with me."

"Well, that's nice! Don't you want me?"

"Hortense, it's not a question of wanting. Of course, I want you. I'm hungry for you—always. But we *could* be under surveillance. Sam has already warned me: *This guy is a rat.* Senator Sam Pickens probably already knows about you."

"You mean, Sam knows?"

"Let's assume everyone knows."

"But how could anyone know? I've *never* been seen—"

"Using your keys, no; but right here in this restaurant, now"—we were at the Royal Arms—"they all know . . . by the way I look at you, the way you turn your head, the way we talk, and most of all, by the

181

way we *don't* talk. That's when they show it—two people in love. They just sit there saying nothing, with a vacant look on their faces. That's it. That tells the world."

"Tells the world *what?*"

"What do you think?"

"Then I may as well come . . . tonight."

"O.K., then . . . I love you."

Mr. Garrett, Sam Dent, and I went downtown in my car, which I left in a parking garage on Constitution. Senator Hood, who was on the subcommittee, had invited us to stop by his office before the hearing so he could "have the privilege of escorting you in." This suited us fine. At 9:30 we were at his office, and he immediately took us into his inner sanctum where he knocked off the amenities and gave it to us straight.

"To begin with," he said, "this undoubtedly is going to be bad. Lloyd is marked up to go, and he may have to go as a sacrifice—"

"Why?" I said. "What does he have against me?"

"Weakness, for one thing. You're an employee."

"And that makes me weak?"

"If he can shake Mr. Garrett's confidence in you—"

"He can't," Mr. Garrett said in that toneless voice of his, causing a warm surge to sweep over me. But Senator Hood cut him off. "I'm giving it to you straight—from Pickens' point of view. He thinks Lloyd's scalp can be had, as a rotten anti-Robert E. Lee, anti-God, anti-motherhood, pro-nigger, and pro-man-eating-shark creep. And he needs a scalp in the worst way. He doesn't dare attack the Institute, which is a project everyone admires. But a worthy project's faithless

182

employee—"

"But, Senator, I have—"

"Lloyd, we have only a few minutes, so let me finish. He's a master cross-examiner, so I beg you, whatever he does, *keep your cool. Don't slug it out with him. Don't for one second try!* He knows all the dirty tricks in the book, and I doubt that you know any. He'll give that crazy writer his head, and—"

"Is *he* going to be at these hearings, too?"

"He'll be the star witness, and he'll be coddled along, encouraged to 'tell it in his own words,' allowed to gabble his head off, so all sorts of things can be put in the record, so Pickens can have them reprinted at government expense and distributed all over Georgia. But when it comes your turn to testify, you'll be put in a straitjacket of 'did you or did you not?'—which will restrict you to yes or no answers. And if there's the least discrepancy between what you say and what somebody else says or between what you say at one point and what you said a few minutes earlier, you're going to hear the word *perjury* until you're climbing the wall with frustration—or worse yet, rage. So, once more, cool it."

Mr. Garrett said: "There may be something I can do."

"I wouldn't count on it," the senator said. "I doubt that you'll get the chance to do anything. You'll be handled with kid gloves as a distinguished, public-spirited citizen whose confidence has been abused by a radical, nigger-loving extremist."

"We'll see."

The door opened and the senator's secretary brought in Miss Snyder, Mr. Garrett's Washington girl who handed him two large manila envelopes. He slipped out what was in them part way, to check them. In one envelope were photographs and in the other what looked like Xeroxes. Miss Snyder whispered to him: "I'll be there at the hearing, behind you, if you need me." This was stuff on Pickens Mr. Garrett had in reserve. As it turned out, it wasn't needed.

Senator Hood waited, then at two minutes to ten escorted us into the committee room which was on the same floor as his office. By then it was full of spectators who eyed us as though we were animals in the zoo. He took us to the chairs reserved for us with a bunch of tables between them and the dais where two or three senators were already seated. Then he left and went up to the dais. In the chair beside me, looking at us sideways, was the writer who had caused all the trouble. Off to one side on tripods were TV cameras and their crews.

Suddenly everyone rose, and Senator Pickens came in. It was the first time I had ever seen him, though, of course, I had seen pictures of him. He looked about the same, except for his color, which didn't show in the pictures: a bright, purple red. Otherwise, in a coarse, John C. Calhoun way, he was impressive enough, with gray hair and craggy, beetling eyebrows. He rapped with a gavel and announced that the hearing was to "inquire into alleged abuses on the part of the Hortense Garrett Institute of Biography, a foundation enjoying exemption from federal taxes." He then called the writer, had him sworn, and after asking his name, place of residence, and occupation, got down to business. I must have tensed, because Mr. Garrett leaned over and patted me on the knee. Once

184

more, I fought off the feeling it gave me—of having a friend who would stand by me through thick and thin.

"The daily papers," Senator Pickens began, addressing the writer, "have reported a conversation between you and Lloyd Palmer, director of the Hortense Garrett Institute of Biography, on or about March 18 of this year. Did such a conversation take place?"

"It did, yes, sir."

"Is Mr. Palmer here in this room today?"

I raised my hand.

"Will you please stand, Mr. Palmer?"

I stood, feeling as though in a pillory.

"Is this the Lloyd Palmer with whom the conversation took place?"

"Yes, sir, it is."

"Will you tell the sense of this conversation?"

That left me standing there, and in a moment I sat down. Apparently, that was what the senator was hoping for.

"Mr. Palmer," he bellowed, "*I* will say when you may sit down. I asked you to stand. You may stand!"

I didn't move.

"Mr. Palmer, did you hear me?"

"Yes, Senator, I did."

"Then why don't you do as I order you?"

"Senator," I heard myself say, "for your information and in case you have forgotten it, I hold the highest rank this country knows: I'm a citizen of the United States. You're not ordering me to stand up, and nobody else is. Upon your *request*, I will stand. I *did* stand. But I will decide when I sit down, not you. I suggest that you remember that. I can't make you do it any more than you can make me take orders from

185

you. I can make you goddam well wish you had."

"Are you threatening me?"

"Yes."

What I was threatening him with I didn't exactly know, but before he could ask me, crackling applause broke out—for me, not him. He turned furiously to the writer and asked him for the second time to give the "sense of that conversation," and the next thing I knew, here it came in a diatribe I could hardly believe. It polished off Douglas Southall Freeman, what a heel he was to accept assignments writing up Longstreet, "knowing all the time that he didn't dare tell it fairly or he would show up Robert E. Lee and what a mess he made of Gettysburg, when he disregarded Longstreet and sent Pickett in anyway and proved what a phoney he was."

"Oh come, come," the senator interjected.

"Senator," this military expert shot back, "Robert E. Lee is the most overrated, overpraised, and overwritten military commander in American history. He fought one great battle—Fredericksburg—which was set up and delivered to him on a platter by a Union general under pressure from Washington. But it was a purely defensive battle. Offensively, Lee had two assets, one named Stonewall Jackson, the other James Longstreet. His one great offensive attempt—Gettysburg—I can prove to you was copied step by step and shot for shot from Joseph Hooker's Chancellorsville plan, which had left Lee doomed before he was saved by Jackson. That's right. I mean to say: Lee copied his whole campaign from the one his enemy had used against him. Yes sir, I said *phoney*, and now, I repeat that word."

"Did you make this point to Palmer?"

"Yes sir, I did."

"And what was Palmer's reaction?"

"He agreed with what I said and told me to go ahead—once I made it clear that I would not be dictated to."

"Did Palmer try to dictate to you?"

"Not in so many words, no."

"Then in what words. Please tell us, if you recall them."

"Senator, he had me down for a hundred a week, and that gave him the right to dictate if I submitted to it."

"And you refused to submit to it, is that right?"

"I did refuse. Yes sir."

"In so many words?"

"In those words."

He repeated himself quite a lot as other senators got in it, each time making somewhat incredible remarks about Lee. At last Senator Pickens asked him to step down, and then the senator called my name. I took the seat the writer had sat in, the one by the microphone, and Mr. Garrett moved to the seat beside me.

To say I was nervous as I took the oath and gave my name would be an understatement. I sounded queer and my voice had a tremor in it. The reason, of course, was that I was terrified at the direction the questions might take. I couldn't be sure that Hortense and I had not been under surveillance, and in spite of lying awake at night, I hadn't come up with anything to do about it. However, I sounded a bit more natural after the first few questions which focused on Harvey's Restaurant and Robert E. Lee.

"Did he or did he not," roared Senator Pickens, "traduce Robert E. Lee to you?"

"He criticized General Lee, yes."

"Stigmatizing him?"

"He took exception to Lee's generalship."

"And what was your reaction?"

"I had none. I'm not an expert on Civil War generalship."

"You did not defend General Lee?"

"Defend him? Why should I have defended him?"

"A great soldier, a great educator, a great man—and you let these slurs be passed on him without uttering one word in his defense?"

"It wasn't up to me to defend him."

"But you accepted this man's characterization?"

"I did not. He didn't tell you the truth. He had some idea—he seemed obsessed with it—that I was trying to dictate to him, to block him from the approach he had in mind, to keep him from writing a biography of Longstreet. I kept telling him that I was not. I told him to write his book as he saw it and if that involved derogatory reflections on General Lee, then that was his conception of it, and the Institute had no objection."

"In other words, you did agree?"

"In no other words but yours, Senator. I told him to write his own book—not my book or the Institute's book or *your* book, for that matter."

"I'll thank you to leave me out of it."

"And I'll thank you not to put words in my mouth."

By this time I was myself. I sounded civil, verging on oily, and my little crack got a laugh. But the senator wasn't done yet. He reverted to his basic theme—that I was a faithless, unprincipled creep who had committed a fine institute to anti-Southern writing with his employer's knowledge.

"Did you or did you not," he asked me, "discuss

this blackening of General Lee's name with Mr. Garrett?"

"Not until you got in it, Senator."

"You withheld it from him?"

"I had no reason to bring it up."

"But you discussed it with Mrs. Garrett?"

"Did I?"

"I am asking *you*, Palmer. Answer me!"

"I thought you were telling me. No, not with her, either."

"You've seen quite a lot of her?"

"Daily, almost."

"Where, Dr. Palmer?"

"At her office, at my office, in the Garrett Building, and lately at our offices in the new Institute building. Also at lunch, and quite often, at dinner."

"And you didn't mention this to her?"

"Again, not until you got in it."

"Not even in your cups?"

"In my *what*?"

He picked up a sheet of paper. "I hold in my hand," he said, "a copy of the restaurant check you paid on the evening of April 13 last, one week ago today—one the waitress pencilled your name on, which shows a fifteen-dollar charge for one quart of champagne. You drank this wine, Palmer?"

"No, I did not."

"You mean to say, *she* did? Mrs. Garrett?"

For a moment my head was spinning around, trying to locate myself on this bottle of champagne and figure out what in the name of God he was getting at. His question, though, gave me a clue. He was getting ready to line me up for more of his basic theme: that I had so little respect for Hortense, I'd get cockeyed drunk at dinner with her, a continuation of what a worthless, respect-lacking employee I was—which, of course, would go down well in the teetotalling parts of Georgia. But mainly, I sensed that he knew nothing of what I had been dreading, which was my relations with Hortense, and my head suddenly cleared. I knew then that I would disregard all the warnings I had had from Senator Hood and let Pickens have it with both barrels, if God gave me the strength.

"No, Senator," I answered quite casually. "Mrs. Garrett doesn't drink."

"Then you drank it, Palmer?"

"No, Senator, I did not."

"Well, somebody must have!"

"I would assume that the couple across the room did, the couple Mrs. Garrett sent the wine to. A girl at the Royal Arms got married week before last and was having dinner that night with her husband. Mrs. Garrett went over to congratulate them and give Lucy a kiss. Then she asked me to order the wine so she could send it over as a gift from her—which I did. She paid me for it . . . which leaves you looking rather silly, Senator."

"Never mind how I look, Palmer. Now did you—"

"Just a moment, Senator; I'm not finished yet."

"I'm asking the questions, Palmer!"

"And I'm giving the answers. Senator, the mistake you made was to bring this subject of alcoholic refreshment up at a hearing you invited TV to cover, which will show on color film a witness named Palmer with the pasty-pale skin of the man who drinks only water, and a senator named Pickens, with a skin of the deep, crimson-red color that comes from only one pot. Senator, all over Georgia tonight they

190

will see with their own eyes, which of us is sober and which the drunken sot!"

He bellowed something, but the roar of applause I got drowned him out. Then he got another surprise. Mr. Garrett was suddenly there on the dais beside him, looking down at him like something carved out of granite. Then the toneless Garrett voice was coming through the mike.

"Senator, you will expunge from the record all references to my wife—*now*. Do you hear me?"

But the woman with the stenotype was already tearing up tape. The applause from the crowd bordered on an ovation, with people standing up. As Garrett came marching back, I was still on my feet, and he was extending his hand. I was so glad to take it that I wanted to cry. That handshake, that warm, wonderful grip, was the greatest moment I ever had, in my whole life, with another man.

21

A croak came over the loudspeaker system: "This hearing's adjourned," and the people were swarming around us, shaking hands and aiming cameras. Then we were back in Senator Hood's office with everyone gloating over what we'd done—Mr. Garrett "for teaching the bastard manners," and me "for really settling his hash—that cooks his goose in Georgia, make no mistake." Well, it did cook his goose, as we know, but I didn't much care at the time. I wanted out of there. Then I found myself down on the street with Mr. Garrett. He was patting me on the back and saying: "Lloyd, as you know, this stuff that Hood peddles—discretion and going along—I'm for most of the time. I practice it myself. But every so often the one thing that fills the bill is a sock on the snoot, and boy, did you give him one today. I'm still exulting over it. I glory in what you did. I can't thank you enough."

Then I was home lying in bed with no idea how I got there. I had to be alone, to face up to this thing in my life, not the clobbering of Pickens, because that was something I had to do but took no interest in. It was that handshake and how it made me feel that I had to face up to now, especially what it meant in my life. One thing was clear, and it kept hitting me: once that handshake was given, once I felt as it made me feel, I couldn't lie anymore. I had to come clean, with no fiddling or foodling or faddling around. So where did that leave me? I wrestled with it, hating to face up to what it was leading to.

Sometime during the afternoon I realized that I hadn't heard from Hortense and thought it very odd. She must have heard about what had happened. It seemed peculiar that she wouldn't have called me. A few other people did, those who had my number, with congratulations for what I had done. But she didn't. Then in the early evening I heard her key in the lock and then she was calling me.

"I'm in here," I called out, sounding thick.

She came in and without saying hello lay down beside me in the dark but without taking off her clothes. I was dressed, too, with the spread pulled over me. There we lay for several minutes, the first time, I suppose, we'd ever stretched out that way. But she acted so strangely that I asked: "Is something wrong, Hortense?"

"Wrong? *I'll* say there is."

Then, almost at once: "Lloyd, it's not that Teddy creature, the one I thought it was. It's *Inga*."

"Who?"

"The housekeeper, the Swedish housekeeper."

"That doesn't make sense."

"It's so, just the same. The woman detective reported today, at last. Lloyd, she got in there by going up in the elevators, the way I told her to, pretending that she wanted a job when Inga came to the door. And when she spoke Swedish, Inga let her in. She had no work for her but gave her coffee and the names of some places she might apply at. Then she apologized for running the woman out, but said her boss was coming and she had to give him lunch. Then when the woman was leaving, Inga called out: 'Oh, no, not here! We have a hideout downstairs, a little place with two rooms where no maid is on duty to see. My boss mixes love with lunch'—and she flipped up her skirt to show she had no pantyhose on . . . Lloyd, how *could* he?"

"Easy, just stretch her out and—"

"It's no laughing matter!"

"I didn't say it was. I just said it's easy."

"Well, if that's how you feel about it!—"

"Ask *me* what's new, why don't you?"

"You? What are you talking about?"

"They had a hearing today. Remember?"

"Oh, *that*."

"Yes, that."

"Well? What happened?"

"I clobbered the senator—and your husband finished him off."

"So?"

"Then we shook hands."

"And the sun stood still—or what?"

"It changes things."

"In what way?"

If she couldn't see in what way, I didn't know how to tell her. I didn't even try. She started all over again, telling me what Inga had said. It seems that there was quite a bit more—how loving her boss was at night, and how he liked *auser*, as Inga called it in Swedish, meaning extra, at lunchtime, for which they needed the hideaway so the maid wouldn't catch them at it. Then she raised up on one elbow and announced:

"Lloyd, I have to *know* what this *means*! I can't fool around any longer, playing it in the dark."

"Nobody asked you to."

"And my waist is an inch bigger than it was this time last week. It's beginning to show!"

"You're six months gone. That's why."

"I have to *talk* to *him*!"

She reached him not at the hotel but at the AR-MALCO offices. It took some arguing to get him to come, but finally she snapped: "Richard, do you think I'm playing games? I said get out here to Lloyd's apartment in College Park—and come now!"

Why it should have bucked me up, I have no idea, but it did. I suddenly felt proud of her—and hope-ful—in spite of what I had to do. As soon as we got up and she made the bed, I got out my personal station-ery and wrote my resignation in longhand.

I addressed it to Mr. Garrett and simply said: "I re-sign as the institute's Director." I wrote it on the cock-tail table in the living room while Hortense was back in the kitchen, fixing bacon and eggs. I went back and we ate. Then we sat in the dark, holding hands, whis-pering, waiting for Mr. Garrett to come. He had said he would be there about ten.

At last Miss Nettie called to say he was there. I put on the lights, opened the door, and waited. When he came, I gave him my hand. He took it again and gave it that extra shake that said that he meant it. When he came in, he kissed Hortense and looked around at the apartment, especially the pictures. At the one of me on my perch as a lifeguard at Ocean City, he snapped his fingers sharply. "I knew I'd seen you somewhere!"

196

he said. "I said so, didn't I, that very first day, when you came to the apartment in Wilmington? Remember?"

"Yeah. But give—what's the rest of it?"

"At Ocean City—I was spending the day there and got interested in this guard, the wigwagging he was doing, and asked him about it. But he corrected me. 'We don't wigwag,' he said; 'we semaphore.' And it turned out that he was semaphoring about a child, a girl in a red dress with white polka dots—"

"I remember now," I said; "and you told me, 'If that's all that's bothering you, there's a red dress under the boardwalks, sticking out of the sand,' and we both crawled under, and there was the lost child. A lot of gratitude we got. Some children get lost on purpose."

"It just goes to show," Hortense said.

"Show what?" he said.

"Well, if you don't know—"

"She's always doing that," he complained, turning to me. "Getting off a real deep thought and then leaving it up in the air, dangling. But it does explain why I remembered you, and you had no recollection of me. You hardly looked at me."

He left the pictures at last, then crossed to a sofa and sat down, facing Hortense. "What's this all about?" he asked her.

"Richard, I want a divorce."

"No."

"I must have a divorce. I'm pregnant."

"I've known you were for some time, knew it before you did, perhaps. Your eyes betrayed you. For several days they had that madonna look they had that other time. The answer still has to be no."

"The answer has to be yes. Richard, I'm going to get

a divorce whether you like it or not; I'm going to get it regardless of what you say."

"You're *not* going to get it. Under the law, you must come to court with clean hands. As far as I'm concerned, you're as clean as baby's breath, but a court—when your pregnancy comes to light—might feel differently."

"How would it come to light?"

"I would light it, that's how. Hortense, I mean *no*."

"Why?" I said.

He didn't answer me or even look at me.

"Did you hear what I said?"

He still didn't answer or look at me. I took my resignation out of my pocket and handed it to him. "Mr. Garrett," I said, sounding pretentious but not knowing how to sound otherwise, "that note will tell you, I think, the depth of my feeling for you, especially after today—what we did to that son of a bitch and the moment it gave us later. I mean the handshake we had. After that, I couldn't play it slick. I couldn't have false pretenses with you. So I wrote this note . . . to get it over with. In spite of all that, in spite of what I feel, I have to tell you that you don't get out of here until you spit it out—what it's all about, why Hortense can't have a divorce. A football player is no more persuasive than anyone else, except for one thing: he doesn't mind playing rough. So, making it as plain as I know how, if it means you stay here all night, here's where you'll stay—until you tell Hortense *why* she can't have a divorce. We know about Inga, so take it from there."

He got up, his face falling apart, apparently stunned. It crossed my mind that it was probably the first time that he had been told what to do, what he *had* to do, by anyone. He took out his handkerchief, crumpled it, and pressed it to the palms of his hands. Then suddenly he said: "I can't stay out of her bed."

"But, Richard, *how could you?*"

Her voice was quavering. Suddenly, instead of talking to me, he began giving out to her. "There's no mystery to it," he told her. "The night you had your miscarriage, I carried you downstairs. Remember? To the ambulance, and rode in it with you to the hospital. Then, when I got in the cab to go back to the apartment, I knew I had strained my back. That's where Inga came in. She had a vibrator, already plugged in by her bed, which she used on herself sometimes. She stretched me out and put it on me. So . . . I spent the night. That's all—or almost all. Hortense, you, of all people should know: I have a hang-up about sex. I don't know why, I just do. She's the only woman I've ever known who really responded to me. As I said, there's nothing mysterious about it."

He trailed off, still talking to her, and then sat looking at nothing while she stared at him for a long while.

"You haven't answered my question," I said. "Why—?"

"Oh. Oh, yes. If Hortense divorced me, Lloyd, I'd be free to marry this woman. I don't think I would, but I might—I'm nuts about her, that I have to admit. I must not, cannot, will not let it happen! If she had stolen a million dollars or murdered someone or danced the hula in church, I don't think I'd mind very much. I could probably tough it out. But marry a servant—no. No, NO!"

He breathed it in a whisper that had the Book of Revelations in it. Hortense got up, walked around, and looked out the window as though thinking it

199

over.

"Yiss," she trilled, "it devolves. It devolves that you smaken me on my pretty Swenska tail whenever I uppen my skurt. But wait, wait, wait unteel I peepen and see if mein pantyhosen iss clean!"

"Goddamn it, knock it off!"

"Now there's a hostess for you! 'Come in, pliz! Yiss, he iss home—aye tink.' " And she popped two or three kneebends which I have since heard are called "knicks," so jerky they make you uncomfortable, while he chased her around, furious. I stepped between them and motioned for her to sit down.

"We get the idea," I said. Mr. Garrett stood for several moments, clenching and unclenching his fists. Then he stalked to the foyer, got his hat and coat from the closet, and put them on. He turned to her and said: "The answer is still no. While Inga is alive, there will be no divorce for you."

"But what am I going to do?"

"Nothing! Nothing. Do that, you will be sitting pretty. *Have* your child—and who knows whose child it is except you, me, and Lloyd? I've told you, it's well provided for. I'm putting it in my will, as well as any other children you have. I'm providing for you in the trust fund that's already set up for you. I dote on you, you must know by now. I feel for Lloyd much as he says he feels for me. You can't have everything, Hortense. All you need do is nothing and you're sitting so pretty, someone should take your picture."

"Except for the one thing I want!"

"I don't. That's the difference."

I went to bed but lay in the dark a long time before she

came in and undressed and presently slipped into bed beside me. But she didn't come close. Then, when I turned on the light, she was staring at me with a strange look in her eyes, as though she were scared to death or had just waked up to something or had gotten a terrific idea—or all three. I made a speech about getting some sleep, how we needed it so we would be fresh in the morning to tackle what had to be done in some kind of clear-headed way. She made no answer, so I turned out the light.

I must have fallen asleep, because all of a sudden I woke up with the feeling that I was alone. I put out my hand. She wasn't there! I turned on the light. Jumping out of bed, I rushed through the apartment, shouting her name; but she wasn't there. She was gone.

I came back to bed and turned out the light. Now I faced a darkness blacker than black. I had lost my job, my dream, and now this woman who had meant so much to me. Yet there is a limit to how much you can feel. By daybreak I didn't feel anything—just cold gray nothingness.

22

For the next two weeks I didn't live. I skulked—alone, seeing no one except people who meant nothing to me, such as parking lot attendants, gas station men, and waiters, and doing nothing but pray she would come back. I'd make my own breakfast, go down and pick up my mail, the paper, and messages, then go out as though I were going to work, the way I always had. I would walk around to the parking lot, have a look at my car, then let myself in the back way and come back up on the freight elevator to the apartment again. Every time the phone rang, I dived for it. Around ten each morning, Eliza would come, make the bed, put out fresh towels, and straighten up; but on Fridays she really cleaned and would be there till midafternoon. So I wouldn't be underfoot, I would go down the back way again, get in the car, and drive—anywhere—Annapolis, Baltimore, Richmond, Frederick, wherever. Then I would come back and at six watch the news on TV. I would go out to dinner, generally the Royal Arms. Then back to the apartment, "to catch up on my reading." But reading just to kill time is the most pointless thing I can think of, and pretty soon, I would turn to cards. Then to bed, for the simple reason that there was no place else to go.

The day after the hearing, Mr. Garrett called to say that Georgia had seen the news stories and that the aftermath was terrific, with editorials in the papers, "and all kinds of beautiful stuff." But no word about my resignation or what his reaction was. Then Sam Dent called to find out where I was. When I told him that I had quit, he was stunned. Then, in no more than a couple of minutes, Mr. Garrett called again.

"What the hell is this, Lloyd? I just read your note, the one you gave me last night. It's been in my pocket all the time. I forgot it completely. What's the point of it? Have I done something? Why are you resigning?"

"That handshake we had did it."

"Did what?"

"It meant I had to end the deception. On my part, sir, that handshake was sincere, and I felt it was on yours, too. So I had to resign."

"What deception?"

"Do I have to draw you a picture?"

"You mean, about Hortense?"

"That's right—about Hortense."

"But, Lloyd, I wasn't deceived, so what deception was involved?" He paused and then said: "Well, yeah, I suppose I flinched a little. But not from what I knew had to be going on. It was how to take it that bothered me. But little by little we all liked each other so well that it was nothing to flinch from at all. You've dreamed yourself up a bugbear that doesn't exist. What the hell. Let me talk to her."

"She's not here."

"Well, she's not at the Watergate apartment. Where is she, then?"

I didn't say anything for a moment, then: "I don't know."

"Say what you mean, Lloyd."

"I mean she's walked out on me—or, at least, I think she has."

"If she wasn't so goddamned headstrong—" He let it dangle, then finished: "She wouldn't be Hortense, otherwise, Lloyd."

"You can say that again."

"Getting back to your note—"

"I'm sorry, sir, it's final."

"It certainly *is* final. I've just burned it in the ashtray. I'm punching the ashes now. Now—will you be in? Can I tell Sam to simmer down?"

"No, Mr. Garrett, I won't be in."

"Lloyd, goddam it, I'm getting annoyed."

"O.K., but I won't change my mind."

"Suppose I find her for you? Suppose I bring her back?"

"Shut up, damn it, shut up!"

"All right, now I know what I have to do."

On Friday when I got in, I rang downstairs to ask Miss Nettie if I had had any calls, and she said no but that I did have a visitor. "That girl who was here before. Rodriguez, I think her name is. She's been here since just after lunch. I said you were out, but she said she would wait."

I told Miss Nettie to give me a moment to think and then said: "Send her up."

But what stepped out of the elevator was a girl I had never seen. In place of the ratty, reddish hair she had had before was a mound of black curls, a little crimson bow on them over one eye; a knee-length black dress, very smart; crimson shoes matching the bow, with high heels and open toes and a mink coat I could hardly believe when I saw it. It was full length, full fashioned, and dark, something a movie actress might have, but not many honest women. She also had a sulky look on her face which was quite different from the crazy, hop-skip-and-jump goof who had been there before. Actually, she looked like the Spanish dame she was, not like some sorority kid cutting up. She inclined her head for a moment and then brushed past me into the foyer, through to the arch to the living room where she stood looking around as though to get reacquainted with something remembered but not remembered too well. Then she took off her coat, spread it over a chair, and stretched out on a sofa to face it—all without saying a word.

"Well," I said, "you again."

"Yeah, it's me."

"What do you want?"

"You."

"You can't have me."

"I know that. You asked what I wanted. I told you."

"O.K., honesty's good for the soul. But if I'm what you want, and you already know you can't have me, I don't get it. Why are you here? I don't want to seem inhospitable, but—"

"In other words, what am I *doing* here?"

"Yes."

"Just . . . looking you over again. Hoping against hope that I didn't like you so much any more. And now that that hope is dashed, how I'm getting the same old buzz, to catch up on you just a little, you and your girl friend—that I don't like even a little bit. Where is she, by the way?"

This caught me off balance, and I sat there not making any answer. Suddenly she jumped up, came partway around the table, and peered down at me. "She hasn't been home for two weeks, that much I already know," she snapped, biting off her words short. "And I know where she is—or was. Do you?"

"Go back where you were."

"I asked you—"

"And I told you."

She went back to the sofa, but didn't lie down. She just sat on it, staring at me.

"O.K., then," I said. "I'll answer you. I don't know where she is. She blew one night. Just disappeared like that. When I went to sleep she was there, and when I woke up, she wasn't. I'd see her in hell before I would lift a finger, before I would pick up that phone to try and find out where she is. So if you know, don't feel you have to tell me. Don't think you'll be doing me a favor. You won't be."

"Where do you think she is?"

"Europe."

I didn't know I was going to say it, but when things reach a certain point, you mean to clam up and don't.

"Europe? What makes you think *that*, Dr. Palmer?"

I snapped: "If she had bought a ticket, that would be a reason. What's it to you why I think it?"

"One of her reasons could be to have her child over there."

"And another might be to find a place to mind her own business in."

"Okay, touché. It's what you said to me one time, when I hadn't even been touched. Remember? Just patted a bit on the patches I had. She *is* knocked up, isn't she?"

"If she were, would I tell you?"

"If she weren't, you would but quick."

I let that one ride and she began again. "Now that I'm caught up on her, at least a little bit, why not catch up on me? Ask me about me. Show some interest, like, where did I get this coat?"

"You might say *how* you got it."

"And you wouldn't like that?"

"Well? Would anyone?"

"But you *wouldn't* like me to say?"

"Put an ad in the paper, why don't you?"

But I sounded the least bit wild, and she got up and came over and looked down at me again. Then in a low, slow whisper: "You care how I got it, don't you? Dr. Palmer, that makes me happier than anything I can imagine! And all the more because I can say it wasn't the way you think it was. Not that it mightn't have been. Not that I'm morally pure. I wasn't trying to be, but I am."

"That's about as clear as mud in a wine glass."

"I was willing, but he was unable."

"What's with that guy in bed?"

"Something—he doesn't know what himself. And *I* sure don't. Except with one woman, he just can't do it. Dr. Palmer—"

"Get back where you were."

She went back to the sofa and went on without any break: "So let's get back to that day when I carried the suitcases for you and he drove me to College Park. We sat in his car for a long time and he got to the point right away—how well he liked me, how pretty he thought I was, how he liked to hold my hand. And so he asked how's about it. And I asked him back—did he mean what he seemed to mean, recreation done in bed in a horizontal position? He said, yes, that was it. At first I held back because of a yen I had for a certain Ph.D. in English poetry, perhaps by the name of Palmer. But then when he said I wouldn't regret it and seemed to mean wordly goods, I screwed up my nerve and asked him if he meant something like a mink coat. And he said yes, he did mean that. I said, O.K., I asked nothing better. In my own mind I was faithless to poetry, English or otherwise, and particularly to a guy named Palmer. Well, I said I was morally pure. Didn't I, Dr. Palmer?"

"Get on with it. What then?"

"At least you're interested."

"Didn't you hear what I said? Get on with it."

"So he called me, maybe a week after that, sent his driver for me and brought me to his hotel, one of the big ones downtown where he'd taken a suite. Did you know, Dr. Palmer, that once you take a suite, you can bring up a girl if you want to, with no questions asked? I thought it was him who was so big they didn't dare squawk, but it turned out that it was the suite. So, anyway, there I was in his arms, holding close, and then he was peeling me off. He peeled me down to the skin, until I had nothing on. I expected results, of course. I mean, like with you that day, Dr. Palmer, there was physiological proof that you weren't indifferent to me—"

"You don't have to go into the details."

"Except maybe I want to."

"Get on with what you were saying."

"There weren't any results—physiological, I mean."

"Hey, hey?"

"No, don't say 'hey,' Dr. Palmer. He's not gay, I

promise you he's not. It's not like that at all. Just the same, he has some mental block about sex—*that* he halfway admitted to me. I mean, he had me do things like walking in front of him, on my hands yet, doing the upside-down split. You know what that does to a girl."

"I can guess, I suppose. And?"

"Even that didn't help."

"What then?"

"At the end of a week, no soap. At last we called it off. That part, I mean. But we had become good friends, and he leveled with me, what it was all about: on account of liking me, he'd hoped I could break him clear of the thrall he was under, he called it. What's a *thrall*?"

"Like handcuffs or—"

"Yeah, I betcha, I betcha!"

She was all excited and went on: "The way he told it, I knew that's what it was like. Dr. Palmer, I think he's banging the Swede!"

"Banging the—"

"Swede woman keeps house for him. I think he's doing it to her morning, noon, and night. I think it's what ails him—that she's got the hex on him so he can't do it with anyone else—even me, willing as I was. Because, don't make any mistake, Dr. Palmer, as little interest as you take in me, I meant business with him. But I didn't, you might as well know, I didn't, I didn't, I didn't!"

"You said it once—you didn't."

"So all God's chillen got thralls. She's his, you're mine, and this Hortense character is yours. *If* she is. Well, is she?"

"You think I would admit it to you?"

"Look, if she's got your child in her belly—"

"*Who says she's got my child?*"

"You do, by the way you act."

"So . . . all God's chillen got thralls."

I guess there was more, but not much that day, because I was jangled, and she was, and I didn't encourage her. Pretty soon she left, but next day she was back and we resumed where we had left off. This day, however, she had on a cloth coat, not the mink one.

"I only wore it yesterday so you could see it just once," she said. "Except when I'm going somewhere, like dress-up at night, I leave it home where I'm living now. I drive to school every day, to the university here, I mean, in the car he gave me. Did I mention that he pays all my college expenses? And set up a trust fund for me? It's just like I made it with sin, except I didn't. I'm pure and undefiled—at least since I met this guy, the one I showed my legs to and would take off my clothes for now if he just said he wanted me to."

"He does, and if you do, he'll kick you out."

"O.K., you don't have to holler."

She explained that at first, when her mother saw the coat, she wouldn't let her in the house. She wouldn't have a daughter living there who had got a coat that way. "It took me an hour to convince her that, though I hand't meant to be pure, I was. So—"

She stretched out and wiggled her toes in her open-end shoes.

"What made you say what you did?" I asked. "About *her*, I mean? What made you think she's—"

"Knocked up?"

"Yes, if you want to call it that."

"That's what her mother thinks."

"You know Mrs. Mendenhall?"
"Yeah, sure. We're friends."
"How did that happen?"

She didn't answer that day or the next or the next, but then one day she did.

"She came to see me, that's how, when I was in Wilmington one time, at the Du Pont Hotel in a suite he got for me. I may as well own up that we had retakes of the attempt he had made before. I think he had the idea that if he could take it easy, have me there convenient, so the urge would come to *him* instead of him going after *it*, things might turn out as he hoped. They didn't, though I stayed up there for some time— a couple of weeks, at least. Why he mentioned me to her—Mrs. Mendenhall, I'm talking about—I have no idea. Maybe as a cover, to pretend that I was the one he was banging instead of this Inga. Anyway, he did mention me, and then there she was on the phone, wanting to come and see me. Curiosity killed the cat. I said, O.K., she could come. What she wanted to know was the dirt on the bash they had, the one the President came to. She was all steamed up, Dr. Palmer, because she hadn't been asked down. So I hadn't been asked either, but, of course, I knew all about it and kind of filled her in. But, then, by a kind of accident, I found out why she hadn't been asked. To show how high-toned I was, I asked her if she would like some tea, and when she said yes, I made her some on an electric grill I had bought. Then, to be really high-toned, I offered her brandy in it, and she said she'd never had it that way, but O.K., she'd like to try it. So I spooned her some brandy in. Then I spooned her some more and some more and some more after that.

212

She got there around three o'clock, and at five I put her to bed so she could sleep it off. Dr. Palmer, she's a really distinguished woman, with a kind of trained-nurse way of talking—which she was before she got married—and a drunk. I call her what she is. I wouldn't have asked her to come, not to a cocktail party the President was coming to. So to that extent, though I hate to admit it, Mrs. Garrett used good judgment."

"Do you still see Mrs. Mendenhall, Teddy?"

"Oh, all the time. We're thick as whipping cream."

"What do you talk about?"

"She does the talking, always, and always about one thing—'Horty,' as she calls her. I suppose she must love Horty, but if she thinks Horty ever did something right, she's never let on to me that she does. She keeps getting off on Horty's 'genius for wrong decisions,' she calls it, her going to Delaware U instead of Vassar, her marriage to Mr. Garrett, her moving out and going to Washington. But I don't think she knows about you. And certainly I didn't tell her. I just didn't care to own up that I had flopped with you."

Then suddenly: "You taking me or not?"

"Taking you? Where?"

"Bed. Where do you think?"

"I thought we'd been all over that."

"Then I'll take myself off—and I guess I won't be back. There's a limit to what I can stand. Being nice about it, lying here dreaming dreams."

She got up and picked up her coat. As I stepped over to help her with it, I got a flash of the beautiful shape inside the pantsuit she had on. For a second I had an impulse. To fight it back, perhaps, I snapped: *"Where is she?"*

"I don't rightly know. But she was in Wilmington, first. Then she went to New York and then came on back to Wilmington. *That's* what his goons report. Mr. Garrett's, I'm talking about. You're goofy about her, aren't you?"

"Well, I've admitted it to you, haven't I?"

"More times than I wanted to hear it."

23

Then back to the cards and the nothingness for several days, maybe a week. One night when I answered the phone, a familiar voice said: "Lloyd?"

"Mr. Garrett!" I croaked, sounding shaky.

"Is Hortense there?"

"No, she's not."

"Where is she? Do you know?"

"I haven't the faintest idea. She disappeared one night, just walked out on me. Since then, I haven't seen her. And you may as well know: I'd see her in hell before I'd lift one finger to find her."

"Lloyd, I *have* to find her."

"O.K., but if you don't mind my saying so, I don't."

"Also, I have to see you. Can you come in tonight?"

"Mr. Garrett, it's true I've done nothing to find her, but at the same time, she might call me, and I feel I should be here in case she does. If it's that important, why can't you come out here?"

"O.K., O.K., I'll do that."

He arrived in less than an hour. I waited for him out in the hall. When he stepped out of the elevator, we shook hands. We went inside and I hung up his hat and coat and followed him into the living room. He wandered around, looking. Then he mentioned that he was just back from Europe, "from Brussels where I was setting up a new outfit to bid on NATO hardware. I shouldn't have gone, with Hortense playing it wild, but when something like this comes up, you more or less have to be there." Then after looking at more pictures, he said: "Lloyd, when I was here before and you threw the headlock on me, I didn't tell you quite all of it. There was no need to, and I left part of it out, a shameful, terrible part. The night Hortense had her miscarriage, I carried her down to the ambulance and went to the hospital with her. But when I got back, I could hardly straighten up, and I knew I had strained myself. Inga was there, of course, so she took over. She brought me back to her room where she had a vibrator already plugged in, and she put it on my back. It was the first I knew what a mean little place we'd given her to live in. But, Lloyd, it had a *smell*. It smelled like her. While she was working on me, that smell was working, too. We just melted together—the first time, the first time in my life that a woman responded to me. It stood me on my ear . . . I'm still standing on it. But she had an ear, too, so she began dreaming dreams—of marrying me. And when I stalled and sidestepped, and waffled and said how tough that would be, how Hortense would never consent, so I couldn't get a divorce, I suddenly knew that she believed me and that soon I would be free."

"Free? How?"

"As a widower, free."

"Could you make that a little plainer?"

"She meant to kill Hortense."

"Are you serious, Mr. Garrett?"

"There's a balcony outside one of the bedroom windows of the Wilmington apartment, and I caught her out there—imagining things! One push was all it would take, and what could anyone prove?"

"What did you do?"

"Fired her, sent her to London and kept on meeting her there. I told Hortense she'd been called back to Stockholm. Then you entered the picture, Hortense moved down with you, and I brought Inga back. But now Hortense is in it again. She was in Wilmington week before last, staying at the Du Pont but seeing Inga at the apartment. Then she went to New York and Inga went with her. Then back to Wilmington, the two of them still together, and then down here to Washington at the Watergate apartment. That's where he lost her tonight, this gumshoe I got to watch her. And that's when I called you on the chance she was here. Incidentally, I gave him your number so he'd know how to reach me in case he had something to report. Oh, I forgot to mention: the Watergate place has a balcony much like the one in Wilmington. Lloyd, I've got the shakes. I feel that something is up, but I'm helpless to do anything."

He stopped talking but kept walking around. I opened my mouth to say it fit what Teddy had told me, but changed my mind.

Pretty soon he sat down on the sofa across from me. I must have showed the strain because he said: "I'm sorry, Lloyd; it's hard for me to realize that someone else—meaning you—can be just as concerned as me. To me, there is only one Hortense—"

"There couldn't be two."

Then I added: "However, what's going through my head right now is an angle you seemed to have overlooked. You're concerned about Inga's interest in

217

balconies. Try that in reverse—for Hortense."

"I don't follow you."

"By one little push, Hortense could also—"

"Jesus Christ!"

"Of course, it wouldn't really be like Hortense."

"The hell it wouldn't. It would be exactly like her."

We sat there awhile, studying our feet. He started to say something, but I held up my hand. I had just heard the freight elevator speak. It was now after midnight and a most unlikely time for anyone to be using that elevator—except one person. It creaked and creaked and creaked. Then it stopped. From the sound it made, I could tell that it had stopped at the seventh floor, my floor. Then came the sound of a key and the door to the hall opened. The person who came in was a dumpy little woman, maybe forty years old, with a halfway good-looking face, a black winter coat, and a little black hat. She was kind of foreign-looking. Behind her, closing the door, was Hortense in her mink coat, without a hat. My heart skipped a beat as the coat broke in front in a way that suggested the bulge of her belly. She led the way into the living room, but when she got as far as the sofas, the other woman stopped and made two "knicks."

So far, Garrett hadn't moved and neither had I. Suddenly Hortense was furious, blazing away at us: "It's customary for gentlemen to rise when ladies enter the room—or *are* you gentlemen?"

"We do get up when ladies enter the room," I said very loudly, "but when idiots enter a room, we're all crossed up. What was the big idea, just walking out like that? Why couldn't you call just once? Didn't you have any money for a phone call? Why?"

"Don't you talk to me that way!"

"It's my place. I'll talk as I please."

"It's my place, too, and—"

"That's what you think, sister."

She screamed, then came charging over in back of the sofa, and began slapping my face from behind. She yelped at Garrett: *Why don't you get up?*

He still hadn't moved. Now he yawned a big phoney yawn which he pretended to hide behind the back of his hand. "I would have got up," he said, "except I wasn't quite sure I was here. Thought perhaps I had died or turned into glass or something or into air like a ghost. No one has spoken to me since they came into this room or even noticed that I exist."

"I did speak to you—just now."

"Oh, yeah, but I mean, to *greet* me. I have feelings, and they're tender, like young asparagus. And—"

"Then hello."

She snapped it out, but Garrett got up. "And hello, yourself," he said with a cold little smile. "What do you want?"

"From you, nothing. We're calling on Lloyd Palmer, so keep out of it, please, until someone asks you in. As to what's going to be said that concerns you, you'd better stick around so you'll know what's going to be done. Then perhaps we'll talk."

"I'll sit down, if you don't mind."

After Hortense had glowered at him for a moment, she turned to me. "Lloyd," she began very dramatically, "will you, for Inga's benefit, repeat what you've said to me, that you want to marry me, that is, if you still want to?"

"This is Inga?"

"Yes, of course it's Inga."

219

"Then why don't you introduce us?"

Shook as I was at seeing her, I was plenty annoyed, and I must have showed it, that she was treating Inga so rudely, not even bothering to introduce her, obviously for the same reason that Garrett had balked at marrying her: she was a servant. As far as I was concerned, though, she was a guest in my home, and there I had rules.

"Well!" she gasped, "if we have to be that formal about it—Inga, Dr. Palmer; Dr. Palmer, Inga."

"Does Inga have a last name?"

"I just told you her name."

"Her *last* name, I said."

Hortense looked blank.

"It is Bergson," Inga said.

"Miss or Mrs.?"

"Miss, Dr. Palmer, it is Miss."

"Miss Bergson, I am honored. Please sit down."

"Sank you, sank you." She got off another knick but remained standing. Apparently, if Hortense couldn't forget what she was and Garrett couldn't, then she couldn't either. I didn't argue about it, but instead stepped back to where Hortense was standing, by the bookcase next to the fireplace.

"Answering you question," I said, "I want to marry you, of course, and the sooner the better."

"Then why don't you marry me?"

"Because you're still married to Mr. Garrett."

"By my choice or his?"

I hesitated before answering, and turned to Mr. Garrett. "Sir," I said very stiffly, "we've shaken hands these last few days, and I've done all I knew how to prove the way I feel toward you. Nevertheless, I have to repeat now what you said to me here in this room the last time this subject came up: you refuse to set her free, to give her the divorce she wants, lest you yourself become free to marry Miss Bergson. You didn't think you would, you said; but at the same time, you feared that you might and that you mustn't let yourself on account of her being a servant. If she'd stolen money or committed some other high crime, you thought you could face that; but a servant you couldn't accept. So you refused Hortense a divorce and promised her that if she sued for one, you would inform the court she was carrying another man's child, my child, to be exact. I think I'm quoting you correctly."

"Richard?"

Hortense barely whispered it, then waited while he turned the color of chalk. In a moment she went on, to Inga: "It's not true, what he's told you, that I'm blocking the divorce, that I meant to be Mrs. Garrett no matter whose child I'm carrying, and that if *he* sues for divorce, I'll break the news to the court, about another woman—you. It's a lie, what he's told you. Are you convinced? Do you believe me?"

"Yiss, Mrs. Garrett. Sank you."

But Mr. Garrett cut in a muffled, queer voice: "Why do you listen to them, Inga, to her or to him? It's all a lie, what she said—and what Dr. Palmer says, too. It is *she* who is blocking *me*, in spite of what's been said. It will all be unsaid tonight when she calls me later to say, O.K., I can sue for divorce but that, of course, she can't deceive a court and will have to tell them about you. That's all it needs, Inga. Now do you know who is lying?"

"Yiss, Mr. Garrett. *You*."

He opened his mouth to say something, but didn't.

221

He just sat there with his face hanging off his cheek-bones while Hortense stared, Inga stared—and I, no doubt, stared. Then very briskly Hortense chirped: "So! Shall we get on with it?"

"Pliz, Mrs. Garrett, yiss."

Hortense stepped past the sofa, the one on our side of the table, sat down on it, opened her bag, and took out what looked like a blank check. Turning to Inga, she said: "Now, we've been to New York. We've talked to Sven, and he's willing to marry you, provided *I* kick in, which I'm willing to do from my own private fortune that my uncle bequeathed me, not from anything out of my marriage. I will pay you a quarter million in cash, $125,000 tonight and the rest when my stocks are sold by brokers in Chester. But there's one small catch, Inga: the check I write you tonight will be payable to Inga Nordstrom, not Inga Bergson."

There was an interruption at this point which really busted things up for a minute or two. Mr. Garrett sprang to his feet, acting downright hysterical, in a way that matched perfectly what Teddy had told me—about what Inga meant to him, the "thrall" she held him under.

"You're not going to do it, are you, Inga?" he said, moving toward her, past the table and then trying to grab her. But she backed away with quick, defensive steps, holding her arm out all the while, like a football player when he stiff-arms a tackler. This went on for a minute or so, with him asking if it was true, what she meant to do, to which she gave him no answer, and if she believed what I had said—to which she kept saying: "Yiss, Mr. Garrett, yiss. I believe. I believe Dr. Palmer. You lie. You lie to me, yiss."

222

"Knock it off," I said to him, "and sit down."

He went back to his chair and Inga to a chair I had pushed up for her, where she stood pursing her lips and swallowing. Hortense, who had watched the chase without saying anything, now turned to me and asked: "May I borrow your pen, Lloyd?"

"Oh, pliz, Mrs. Garrett, take my."

Inga was unzipping her bag and reaching inside it. But what she came up with wasn't a pen. It was a gun, a snubnosed, shiny thing, the kind known as a "Saturday night special." She raised it, first dropping her bag on the chair, and aiming at Mr. Garrett.

"Now, sir, die—pliz," and she popped him one last knick.

The gun spoke with the deafening roar of a shot fired indoors. There was a streak of yellow light and a sudden billow of smoke. He stood for one last moment, then vloomped down on the cocktail table and rolled onto the floor.

Hortense ran around, dropped down on her knees beside him, and began talking to him in low, vibrant tones. "Richard, Richard; no, no, no—don't go; don't let yourself. No, it's me. Look at me. Oh, darling, darling, darling—"

There was more of this, what I would have wanted her to say and yet hated to hear, hated to overhear because of the intimacy of it. So as not to intrude, not to see such a personal moment, I turned away and glimpsed Inga as she stood there with the gun at her side, seemingly in a daze. Hortense went on and on. Then the change in her voice told me that it was all over, that Mr. Garrett was dead. Then her voice came, hard, bitter, and rasping: "You rotten little—"

But the way she broke off alerted me, and I wheeled

223

around to see Inga aiming once more, this time straight at Hortense. Her back was to me, and I reacted automatically, as quickly as God would let me. I aimed a karate chop at that short little neck. It cracked as she collapsed at my feet, but the gun cracked first—and there was the love of my life, her eyes glazing over yet seeking me and at last finding me.

I reached her in two jumps and caught her before she fell. I had read somewhere that a person suddenly wounded should be stretched out flat and not prodded or twisted or lifted except by trained medical people. I pushed the table over to make room for her on the floor and then eased her down. I grabbed a pillow from a sofa and pushed it under her head, all the while speaking to her. She would answer, not by saying anything but by moving her head just a little as if she were trying to nod. I couldn't see where she was shot, so there was nothing else I could do.

"Darling," I said, "I have to call—call for an ambulance so we can get you to a hospital. I'll be right back."

She moved her head once more, and I sprang for the phone. By then, of course, Miss Nettie had left for the night and I hardly knew the night watchman. He was so dopey when I told him to get the police, so slow to snap out of his sleep, that I slammed the receiver down and called the police myself on the outside phone. I found the number on the emergency list the phone company prints in the front of the book.

"For God's sake," I said, "step on it, will you? There's a woman here who's been shot, and she can be saved if you—"

"Take it easy, pal," said the voice at the other end.

"We'll be there. We're on our way right now."

I opened the hall door and then went back to Hortense. I kept talking to her, but her hand found mine, telling me to be quiet. So, for an eternity, we communed, hand in hand.

24

All of a sudden the elevator door clanged open, there was a knock at the door, and the state police were there, three or four of them headed by a sergeant. There was also an ambulance crew in green smocks, two orderlies and a doctor who looked like a high school boy. He pushed through the officers, knelt by Inga, and immediately fanned his hand to indicate that she was dead. He told the orderlies to lay her out. Then he stepped over to Mr. Garrett, fanned his hand the same way, and motioned to the orderlies again. He knelt by Hortense, felt her pulse, lifted an eyelid with his thumb, and said to the orderlies: "Never mind them. Help me get her down to the ambulance— *now*." He gave the table a kick and they lifted it over the sofa to the space between it and the bookcases, which made room on the floor beside her. Then the doctor took a blanket from a pile the orderlies had brought and put it down beside her, folding it carefully. He pushed one edge of it under her and rolled her on her side. Then he rolled her back, pulled the blanket through, and motioned for the orderlies. They put down the stretcher and lifted her onto it with the blanket.

"O.K.," he said, and they moved her quickly to the elevator. "Hold it," he called and then said to the sergeant: "I have to rush her over if she's going to have a chance. Get your names and the information on the others, and I'll meet you at the hospital in the morgue and sign the certificates for you. They'll both be autopsy jobs, but that report, of course, will be separate."

"O.K., doc, take her away."

Through the door I could see her as they took her onto the elevator, her face pale as the light shone down. She was beautiful. When she was gone, I turned to the officers who had taken up where the orderlies had left off, laying the bodies out for another ambulance crew and covering them with blankets. The sergeant, who said his name was Herbert, sat down on a sofa and motioned to me. The whole place seemed very odd to me now; everything was askew.

"Just a minute while I straighten up," I said. I picked up the table and put it back in place and then pulled the sofa straight.

"O.K.," the sergeant said, "let's go."

"Go where?"

"Suppose you tell me what happened here."

"Well, there's not much to tell, really. Miss Bergson—the woman over there, Miss Inga Bergson—shot Mr. Garrett, the man lying beside her, and then shot Mrs. Garrett."

"Do you know their addresses?"

"I think I do."

"O.K., but first, who shot *her*?"

"Who?"

"Miss—Berson. Is that what you said her name is?"

"No one shot her."

228

"Then how come she's dead?"

"Search me. I didn't know she *was* dead until that doctor said she was. I must have broken her neck."

"You must have—"

I explained what I had done. It took him a moment to readjust. Until then, he had assumed that Inga had also been shot.

"I came down on her neck with my hand," I said, "with kind of a karate chop. But the gun went off first. And when I saw that Mrs. Garrett was hit, I didn't pay much attention to whether Miss Bergson was hurt— and I completely forgot the gun."

He motioned toward the dispatch case he had put on the opposite sofa, saying: "I have it. It was on the floor beside her. So let's go back to the names."

"Wait a minute."

It left me sick to my stomach to realize that I had killed someone. When I told the sergeant, he said: "Take your time. We've got all night."

"No! Maybe you have, sergeant, but I don't." I snapped out of it then, telling him to make it quick, because I had to get to Cheverly to the hospital to find out how Hortense was.

"Calm down," he said; "cool it. One thing at a time. You're the only one who knows what happened, and I have to make a report. So—first things first. Names, please, addresses, and occupations, if you know them. First, this dead guy here—"

I gave him the Garretts' names and the Wilmington apartment as their address, for him and for her, with the Watergate also for her. He said: "Wait a minute. You can't live in two places at the same time."

"You can if you're rich enough."

For the first time, he reacted to what he'd just written down. "Hey!" he exclaimed. "Those names were in the paper. They gave a party. The two of them gave it together, and the President came. Are these the same Garretts?"

"They gave a party, yes; and the President came."

He looked at me and then at his notebook. "When did these people arrive tonight?" he said.

"I don't know. I didn't keep track."

"Wait."

He went to the phone and called the night watchman and questioned him. When he came back, he said: "Mr. Garrett got here at 11:52, but no women came, the night watchman says."

"They must have used the rear entrance."

"What rear entrance is that?"

I told him about the door from the parking lot, which was one floor down from the lobby, and about the freight elevator.

"Does that door stand open?" he said.

"No, I think they keep it locked."

"And these women had a key?"

"Mrs. Garrett probably did, yes."

"What for? So she could get in your place?"

"That's right. She borrowed it sometimes, to use the phone or whatever, and I gave her a key."

"O.K., get on with what happened, Mr. Palmer."

"I thought I had already told you."

"Well, I don't—I don't think so at all. Listen, if you clunked a woman and broke her neck to keep her from killing somebody, it's all right with me and it's all right with the law. I'd have no reason to hold you—provided you come clean. Now, you can have counsel if you want, and plead the Fifth, if you want—but only on the grounds that what you say might incriminate

230

you. Would it?"

"Not that I know of."

"Then you'll have to talk. So get started."

"Give me a minute to get it together."

"Take your time."

I began ticking it off, beginning with my first meeting with the Garretts. He sat looking at me, and then I realized that I was talking into a recorder which he had placed between us. I kept on and on, working down to Mr. Garrett's arrival and what he had come about, his fear that Inga might push Hortense off a balcony. Then I brought the two women in, explaining that they had come without knowing Mr. Garrett would be there. Then I told him about the argument we'd had, trying to keep it brief but, at the same time, clear. I got to the shooting and my jumping at Inga, and finally that seemed to be it. He seemed satisfied.

"O.K., Mr. Palmer," he said very respectfully, picking up the recorder. "I'll ask you to come with me now while I get this down on paper. We'll have to go to the police office in the County Building where I have a typewriter."

"I have a typewriter here."

"You do? Then, if I can borrow it. . . ?"

"Be my guest. I'll get it."

I didn't use it much, and it was in the spare bedroom. I got it for him and he set it up on the table, then started his recorder. So I wouldn't hear my voice croaking at him, I wandered back to the bedroom I had shared with Hortense and lay on the bed in the dark. Then I heard someone come in and went out to find more police and orderlies there to take the bodies away. They made it quick, and then I was there with the sergeant who was still pecking away at the type-

231

writer, accompanied by my voice. I went back to the bedroom. After awhile he called me. He seemed to be through and was studying what he had written.

"What do you do with it now?"

"Turn it in, of course."

"Will newspaper reporters have access to it?"

"Well, that's the whole idea. Under the law, they have the right. When copies are made of it, one will hang on a hook in the clerk's room there in the County Building. Anyone can look, including even them."

"You don't seem to like them much."

"Does anyone?"

He asked me to check it over "for facts," so I had to read it. It was all there in police lingo, from my first call on the Garretts to the doctor's pronouncement of death, with the "intimate relations" between Garrett and Inga precisely spelled out. But one thing I managed to hold back. If he suspected it, he didn't show it, and that was the "intimate relations between Mrs. Garrett and me." That wasn't in the report, thank God, and when I had read it, I said to him: "Fine. It looks O.K. to me."

He got up to go, telling me to stand by, "in case," meaning don't leave town till the case is wound up. Then he left. I sat for a minute and then went downstairs, got in the car, and drove to Cheverly where the Prince Georges General Hospital is.

The girl at the window spoke to me by name. "Do I know you," I said to her.

"Not really, I suppose, Dr. Palmer. I was in your poetry class a couple of years ago, just for three days, till I switched my course. But I remember you well. What can we do for you?"

I said that I had come about "Mrs. Garrett, Mrs. Richard Garrett, to inquire how she is and see her if that's permitted at this hour."

"Well, I'm afraid it wouldn't be—" running her finger over a memo of some kind. "Oh, here she is—yes, she's in Intensive Care. Her condition, unfortunately, is critical."

"Thank you. When can I see her?"

"At two this afternoon—for ten minutes, if, if the doctor will let you see her at all."

25

I drove home and put in a twelve-o'clock wake-up
with Western Union. Then I went to bed and when the
call came, got up. In between, I guess, I slept, at least
some kind of way. When I'd dressed, I went down to
the lobby, picked up the paper, and read it, at least the
high spots. It was all over page one and a couple of
pages inside, with pictures of me, Hortense, and Mr.
Garrett. But none of Inga, I suppose because they
didn't have any. When you're a servant you don't
even have a picture of yourself in the files if you kill
someone. And there was no mention of my relationship with Hortense beyond my being the director of
the Institute, my resignation not having been announced yet. My being—or supposedly being—director of the Institute was the only explanation offered
for the visitors I had at one in the morning. "Refusal
on Mr. Garrett's part to accept divorce and marry
Miss Bergson" was the explanation for the shooting,
according to the papers.

It took about twenty minutes to skim through. All
during that time, Miss Nettie said nothing, although
we were pretty good friends. But when I got up
to go to the hospital, she said: "Quite a time you

had last night."

"You can say that again," I grumbled.

"I want to hear all about it."

"I'll tell you, but not now, if you don't mind. I'm not in the mood for talk."

"Oh that I can well understand."

At a quarter to two that afternoon, I was back at the hospital, talking to another nurse and getting the same report. "She's in Intensive Care. Her condition is critical. You can visit for ten minutes if the physician in charge permits it." So, following directions, I took an elevator, went down a long corridor, and found myself at a door with a dozen people in front of it. They were waiting while a nurse stood there with a card in her hand. When I stopped, she asked who I wanted to see, glanced at her card, and said: "You may stay ten minutes. Stand over there, please." And she motioned for me to go back to the end of the line, and there I went. But a woman had looked up when I mentioned Hortense's name, and now she came up to me.

"You must be Dr. Palmer," she said. "Horty's spoken of you, and your picture was in the papers."

I kept wondering who she was, then a bit grandly, she said: "I'm Mrs. Mendenhall, Horty's mother."

So I knew who she was at last, and I also knew the reason for the pink complexion after what Teddy had told me. But I played up to her, assuring her: "Oh, yes, of course; Hortense has mentioned you often. How is she?"

"Critical, is all they'll tell you, which sounds bad, and I guess is. The paper's not much help. She was still in surgery when they went to press."

"We'll keep our fingers crossed."

"It's all we can do."

We stood there for another dead ten minutes on a day that had seemed all dead. I had not had any breakfast, which may have been one reason I felt so dull. And, of course, I was numb from loss of sleep and the reaction to what had happened—or lack of reaction, actually, as part of my trouble seemed to be that I couldn't quite get caught up on where I was. But not *knowing* where I was was partly the reason for that. I couldn't possibly know until I knew something about Hortense's condition. So I stood there, first on one foot and then on the other.

At last the door opened and a nurse was whispering to the nurse standing with us. Then one by one, after checking against the card, they led us into a large room with beds head to the wall, a doctor walking around, and another nurse directing us. She said something to Mrs. Mendenhall and led us to a bed at one side halfway down the room, and finally we were with Hortense—if the wraith in the bed was her. I hardly knew her, she was so pale. Her hair was combed out in a strange, unnatural way, she had a hospital jacket on, and tubes led down to her arms from bottles above her head. Mrs. Mendenhall whispered to her: "Horty, it's your mother, and here's Dr. Palmer."

She patted one of Hortense's hands, and I patted the other. She didn't open her eyes, but I could tell that she heard what we said and felt what we did.

"We're pulling for you," I said softly; "I love you."

"Yes, we both do," Mrs. Mendenhall said.

That made a family matter out of something I meant as personal; but I let it pass. Then a doctor came by holding his watch up at us, and we left after whisper-

237

ing: "See you tonight." Then we were out in the hall. I told Mrs. Mendenhall that I hadn't had breakfast and asked her to join me. But she said she had to get on to Watergate and "get myself organized there. They caught me in Chester with it. I can't say I was much surprised, since Richard was playing with fire, as I, for one, tried to tell him. Yet when a thing like this happens, it's like bricks falling on you. I drove straight here; I haven't even been to the apartment."

She seemed to know where we were going, and I went along without paying much attention, down a flight of stairs and along a hall to a large window with a lighted room behind it. She tapped on the glass and a nurse appeared inside. The nurse disappeared, then came back pushing a bassinette. Then we were staring down at a tiny, sleeping infant under a blue blanket.

"He's simply beautiful," Mrs. Mendenhall said. "The spitting image of Richard."

To say I was stunned would be the understatement of my life. I suppose, little by little, my mind caught up with what this woman had known, that before surgery could be performed to remove the bullet, this baby had to be taken out. My mind also caught up with the remark she had just made about the child's resemblance to Garrett, which seemed to say that she had no idea of its relationship to me. I still stood there. Suddenly she said "Be back" and fluttered down the hall. Then she was back, but a whiff of her breath told me what she had been doing, no doubt from a flask in her handbag, in the ladies' room.

26

That night was a repetition of the afternoon, but the next day at two, I was there again in line outside the door of Intensive Care. In a minute here came Mrs. Mendenhall in a neat, navy-blue dress that showed off her very good figure, which was much the same as Hortense's but, if I do say so, it was perhaps a little better on the fine points of curve and proportion. She certainly wasn't bad-looking. She walked down the hall and for the first time gave me some of the dope on what the surgeon had been up against while probing for the bullet and performing the Caesarian to deliver the child.

"The shock was simply frightful," she said, whispering professionally. Then I remembered that she had once been a nurse. "He had to handle the whole small gut, letting it slip through his hands and closing each perforation as he came to it. But the real crisis will come in three days—from peritonitis. What leaked out of the gut, of course, fouled the whole abdominal cavity, and there's no way of cleaning it adequately. The surgeon did the best he could. Only time will tell. Her temperature will mount and mount; it will simply be a test of her strength."

"If you don't mind, I've got the idea."

We went in. It wrung my heart to see the shape Hortense was in. Her temperature had gone up, anyone could see that, and she kept whimpering when we touched her in a pitiful, frightened way. Then we were out in the hall again and down to the nursery. Mrs. Mendenhall kept talking about the baby's resemblance to Mr. Garrett, though what resemblance it bore to anyone, including me, I couldn't for the life of me see. To my eye, it wasn't an infant that stirred me to my heels. It just looked like an infant.

We went our separate ways and met again that evening. This time, it turned out, her car had to go in the repair shop to have its right turn light fixed, so she arrived in a cab. So when we left, I ran her over to Watergate, and when she asked me up, I went. I seemed to dread being alone.

It was the first time I had been to Hortense's apartment, and it gave me an odd feeling. It was full of pictures—of Hortense, of Mr. Garrett, of Mrs. Mendenhall, and of me, mostly in football attire, with the bare brisket showing.

We were hardly in the door, though, before Mrs. Mendenhall said: "I simply have to get out of these clothes and into something comfortable. If you'll excuse me." And she disappeared, going out through what looked like a dining room beyond a large arch. Then "Woo-hoo" came her voice. "You could keep company, Dr. Palmer."

I decided it was time to leave.

When I took my place in the hall one day, the nurse beckoned to me. "She's been moved," she said and gave me the new room number. I found my way there and tapped on the door. Mrs. Mendenhall came out.

"She's better," she whispered. "The fever's down and she's well past the crisis, but she's horribly depressed. She keeps talking about her baby, the one she thinks she lost. We haven't told her yet, the way things turned out—thought the surprise would be nicer if we took her down to look and then all in one swoop, she'd see what we've been saving for her."

I agreed that it was a nice way to handle it, and we went in. Hortense hardly noticed that I was there.

"I'm just a thing," she wailed. "Not a woman at all anymore. Just a thing that looks like a woman but isn't any more. My sweet little baby, the last one I can have. They took it from me that night. It's not in me any more. I can feel with my hands: it's not there. And I can never have—"

She kept it up until I motioned Mrs. Mendenhall. "O.K., Horty," she said, "you'll feel better in a moment. We're taking you out for a ride. A little ride around so you have a change. Now, isn't that going to be nice?"

"All right," Hortense said listlessly.

The nurse instructed her carefully after pushing up the wheelchair on what she was to do: lock her hands on her neck and hold on while the nurse lifted her. "And then—"

"Hold it," I said. "I have a better idea."

I peeled the covers down, sat beside Hortense, put one arm around her back, the other under her knees, and lifted exactly the way I lifted her that first time when I had carried her back to the bedroom from my living room. It worked fine again. I slid her down in the chair with no trouble, hoping for a pat or smile or kiss—or something, at any rate, something that

241

would tell me that she remembered. All I got was nothing. The nurse wheeled her out in the hall where Mrs. Mendenhall and I joined them, and off we went, to the elevator, with the nurse pushing Hortense down the hall toward the window of the nursery I had come to know so well. When we were almost to it the nurse stopped, leaving Hortense in the chair, and skipped ahead to the window where she tapped. The other nurse nodded and disappeared. Then our nurse came back and pushed Hortense to the window. The nurse inside was there, pushing the same bassinette. Mrs. Mendenhall said: "O.K., Horty, there's the big surprise we've been saving for you. You didn't lose your child. They saved it and here it is, right in front of your eyes. There he is—your little son."

Hortensed just stared.

"Isn't he beautiful?" And then as she had said twenty times: "He's the spitting image of Richard."

"Oh, for Christ's sake, Mother," Hortense snapped, "he's not Richard's child; he's Lloyd's. Be your age, will you?"

Mrs. Mendenhall shot a look at the nurse and then said quickly: "Horty, in this hospital, he's Richard's— or he'd better be, if you know what's good for you and for him. He's registered as Richard's, and any move on your part to change that is going to raise a stink that will last *his* whole life. So, unless you want to ruin it—"

"All right."

Our surprise was a bit of a flop.

When we got back to the room, Sam Dent was there. At first Hortense seemed glad to see him, smiling a bit when she told him to turn his back as I lifted her back in bed. But after some friendly moments, while he asked how she was and she told him, "well as can be expected," it all exploded once more when he half-cleared his throat and began: "Hortense, as soon as you're able, I'd like for you to read some papers and stuff like that. One or two things have come up—"

That was as far as he got. She didn't even let him finish, screaming at him in a weak voice that sounded all the worse for being so ghostly.

"Do you have to pester me now? Do I have to beg for consideration? Do you know what it means to be shot by a lunatic, to have a child taken out of you, to lie at death's door for five days—"

"Three weeks," Mrs. Mendenhall said.

"To have a foot in the grave the better part of a month? Do you think I can turn around then and begin reading stuff you bring me? So you can get on with some job?" There was more, but Mrs. Mendenhall and the nurse kept trying to calm her down, and Sam kept saying, "I'm sorry, Hortense; forget it. I didn't mean to upset you." When he and I were out in the hall, he tried to explain why he was bothering her about business at a time like this.

"Lloyd," he said, "I had to. Legally, she's it. She's the only one who can say what goes on this stuff that keeps coming up, that's going to keep *on* coming up. Since Mr. Garrett didn't leave any will—"

"He *didn't*? I thought he did."

"He kept talking as though he had, and he certainly meant to, but as far as he got with it was one of those clipboard jobs that he was so fond of—a memo to me about what he meant to put in it. And it leaves her in complete control. There's things we don't dare do without an O.K. from her. Like the debentures on the motorbikes. It's a way to get working capital, but they can't put them out until she signs the order."

"Does she know about the notes?"

"I gave her a copy of them. It was a memo to me, so I had to keep the original. That's part of what's bugging her, maybe. I've thought since then that perhaps I shouldn't have done it. But I had to if she wanted to do what he wanted—I mean, carry out his wishes."

"What's the rest of it?"

"You mean, why I shouldn't have given it to her?"

"Yeah, I'd be curious to know."

"Does the name Teddy Rodriguez mean anything to you?"

"Yes. Teddy's a very close friend."

"He meant to leave her a million."

"Ouch."

"But I had to show it to her—if she wanted to carry out his intentions, as she kept saying she did, whether he made a will or not."

"What other bequests were called for?"

"Million to me, million to you, million to Mrs. Mendenhall, million to the child if, as, and when born, five million trust fund for Inga, to cease upon her death. But without any will to go by, it's Hortense—and she has to make decisions, or else some of these companies that ARMALCO is made up of are behind the eight ball."

"I get the picture."

"He slung millions around like popcorn."

"He *meant* to sling millions around."

"Yeah, sure—correction noted."

27

Next day Sam was back with another nut for her to crack. It seemed that Sol Novak, of Novak Bros., a subsidiary in Akron, wanted to incorporate, but had to have her O.K.

"It's important for ARMALCO protection," Sam told her, "because the partnership, as it stands, is a two-for-one thing, two shares to Sol for every share for his brother, Al. Maybe it's for straight, on the up and up; but maybe Sol's gypping Al. We can't leave things to chance. On our end, we can't have anything out of line or we're wide open if we get sued. So, much as I hate to bother you, Hortense—"

She didn't answer, at least in words. All she did was scream. Just open her mouth and let out ghastly bleats, one after the other. But they got fainter and fainter until she was gasping them out. Then she subsided a bit.

"I see it now," she said. "It's all clear. It means I have to die. Whom the gods would destroy, they don't make mad any more. They let them dream and then make the dream come true. I had that dream every night. I got so I knew it by heart, knew what was coming each time. He was dead; my husband was dead.

And I was the richest woman on earth. I had a yacht like Jackie Onassis's, a mansion like Jane Du Pont's, a coat like Frances Vanderbilt's. I could have whatever I wanted just by waving my hand, *anything* I wanted, anything at all. Then, pretty soon, I would wake up and he would be in the other bed, snoring. But during the dream I was happy, so happy I wanted to fly!"

"Horty, stop talking like that!" Mrs. Mendenhall cut in. "You know that's not true at all. You never dreamed things like that!"

"*I know what I dreamed!*"

"Let her talk!" I snapped. "if she's to have peace with herself, she has to."

"Debentures—what are they? And *corporation*. I don't even know what *that* is!"

"*In*corporation," Sam corrected.

"Incarceration—of me, why don't you say? Well, why don't you? I'm the prisoner of my dream, and it's going to kill me. Oh yes; I know what's in store for me."

It went on and on but at last ran down from her getting exhausted and shutting up. Then Sam and I once more walked out in the hall. A bench was there and we sat down, he mopping his brow which was wet. Then he broke out: "So she dreamed he was dead, so what? We knew that, and it didn't bother her then. She just thought it was funny."

"How do you know what she thought?" In spite of myself, in spite of liking Sam, I sounded a little peevish.

"All I know is what she said."

"To you? She discussed her dream?"

"No, not to me. To her mother. And Mrs. Mendenhall, at a certain stage in her day, talks. She kept dreaming Mr. Garrett was dead, and that made her filthy rich."

"There's no law against it that I know of."

"And there's no reason for it—except one." I didn't ask him what reason. I was afraid to. But he saved me the trouble. "She wanted him dead," he growled.

That kind of put an end to the discussion, at least of Hortense's dream. Perhaps to change the subject, Sam asked me: "When are you coming to work?"

"Work?" I said. "What do you mean, *work?*"

"For the Institute. Well, you started it, didn't you? And you picked Davis who's making a God-awful mess of it. He's got the while place in an uproar. All he knows is one scheme after the other. He's a born troublemaker, not fit to run anything. So, when are you coming to work?"

"I haven't been asked yet."

"*I'm* asking you."

"And you're in charge? That's news to me."

"O.K., you win. The one person in charge, I'm afraid to ask, God help me. It's come to that. She's the only one who can say, and saying something might kill her."

"Listen, she's still desperately ill."

"That's not all she is."

He sat shaking his head, but we both knew we weren't telling it like it was, or any part of what it was. The whole story, the reason she'd popped out with the dream and all the rest of it, was told by the line, "to Teddy Rodriguez, one million." We sat there for some time, not talking about it. Then I popped out with what was bugging me, sort of crying on his shoulder, as he had been crying on mine. "Sam," I said, "what's got into her? All right, she's ill. She's weak from what happened to her. She's not herself. That we know. But it started before that. It started the night he told her, the night Mr. Garrett let her know where she got off, that she couldn't have a divorce and told her why. That night she disappeared. I fell asleep with her beside me, and when I woke up she was gone. Since then, things haven't been the same. She doesn't even know me, not the way she did. Something's gnawing at her more than the dream she would have—in Wilmington, remember. Once she met me, she didn't have any such dream, that I promise you."

"It was handled wrong—the child."

"How do you mean, handled wrong?"

"Keeping the news from her. That was Mrs. Mendenhall's idea. At a certain time of day, Mrs. M. isn't very bright. She should have been told right away."

"It was handled O.K."

"Oh? You think so?"

"She shouldn't have been told."

"You mean, her condition wouldn't have permitted it?"

"She was barely conscious, Sam."

"Then, I take it back."

"Something's griping her."

"By the name of Teddy Rodriguez."

"Yes."

This went on for several days, her talking about the dream, how it gave her no peace, how it was going to kill her. Then all of a sudden, she harpooned me with it.

"So they want you back!" she screamed. "Why don't you *go* back, then? What's stopping you? They'll pay you enough, won't they?"

248

"O.K.," I said after a moment. "Since you put it that way, I have to think about it. I did start it; that's true. I did persuade Mr. Garrett to name it for you. I'll let you know."

"Name it for me? I'm talking about ARMALCO!"

"ARMALCO? I don't get it."

"You could be president of it! You could take him off my back—that Sam Dent. He's sitting right there. You could tell me what I think, and then I could tell *him*. You could, if you had any consideration."

"Who says I could be president of ARMALCO?"

"My husband did—Mr. Garrett."

"*He* told you? That I am fit to be president of—?"

"Do I have to shout? Are you deaf? He did nothing but talk about how smart you were and how he had 'plans for you' and—"

"I have to think about it."

"There's one condition, though."

Sam looked at me. I said: "No conditions, Hortense. If I'm to be president of ARMALCO and tell you what you think, I'll make the conditions, not you."

"*I'll make them!* I'll make them."

"We're back to Teddy Rodriguez," growled Sam, in the hall as we walked to the elevator."

"You think she's the condition?"

"You're to knuckle under after accepting the presidency of ARMALCO and refuse to pay that million. It'll be her way of handling Teddy—and of handling *you*."

"I don't hold still too well for handling."

"For *your* million and that job, you might."

28

A few days later I got a call at the apartment from Mrs. Mendenhall, telling me: "We bailed out of the hospital. We thought, if we paid for both beds in the room or at least were willing to pay, she could have it to herself, but for some reasons that was impossible, and when they moved another woman in, we decided we'd better get out. So we did. And here we are back in Watergate."

"I'll be in—that is, if I'm invited."

"But, Lloyd, of course."

I drove down, parked in the basement, and went up. Letting me in, making knicks, was a girl who looked familiar. I realized it was Karen, the one who let me in on my first call to Mr. Garrett in Wilmington. Mrs. Mendenhall was there, as was a girl named Winifred whom I'd never seen but who turned out to be Hortense's Wilmington secretary. And the baby was there with a nurse, a different one from the one who'd been with Hortense, in the hospital. She sat next to the baby's crib. Next to it was a small table with nursing bottles on it and next to that was a refrigerator. And, of course, Hortense was there. She didn't look up when I went in, but instead lay on a lounge chair while everyone sat around watching her, not speaking. She didn't speak or respond in any way when I gave her a pat. No one asked me to sit, but I sat anyway—and waited. Nothing happened. Sam Dent came in. After she ignored him, he tiptoed to a place near me and sat down. Still, nothing happened. They all just sat there, and so did she. Suddenly I began getting annoyed. I got up, planted myself in front of her, and said: "It's customary among people with manners for the hostess to speak, to make some kind of gracious remark, so people can relax, talk, and act natural."

"Are you instructing me in manners?"

"I'm batting you one in the jaw if you don't say something."

"Like what, for instance?"

" 'Nice weather we're having,' will do."

"Do? For whom?"

"Spit it out, goddamn it, or—"

I stepped in and meant to let her have it whether she was weak or not, whether or not Sam tried to stop me—which he seemed about to do as he jumped up and stepped in between. But she whimpered: "Please, please, please!"

"That'll do," I heard myself growl. "I wouldn't quite call it friendly, but at least we could call it speech—of a human kind."

"Sam! You're not going to let him—"

"I'm stronger than Sam. Remember my thick neck."

"Oh, they called you the Brisket, didn't they?" Mrs. Mendenhall said. "Someone was telling me. *Horty* was telling me. It *was* you, Horty, wasn't it?"

"Mother, that'll do."

For some moments, then, conversation languished. Then Sam Dent cleared his throat and, perhaps to change the subject, got to what he had come about: the naming of cabin cruisers, at the yards up by the Delaware Water Gap. "If you have any ideas about it, Hortense," he said, "I'd certainly be glad to—"

But she exploded once more; "You're trying to kill me, that's what! And you may very well succeed."

"Hortense, nobody's trying to do anything but what has to be done by law. Now if you want someone else to take over, if you'll give him power of attorney—"

"I don't want *anything* but peace!"

"Then O.K., but first—"

She screamed at him again, not words, just screams, and I could see him fighting back whatever it was that wanted out of his mouth. He was usually one of the friendliest guys in the world. But now he seemed to have reached the point where he'd had about all he could take. What he might have said, she didn't hear because just then the phone rang and Winifred went to answer it. She came back, leaned over Hortense, and said something. Then Hortense turned to me. "I asked Miss Rodriguez to call," she said, "on a business matter we have, but she couldn't make it today. May I impose on you, then? Would tomorrow be all right?"

"No imposition," I answered. "Tomorrow's fine."

"Around two?"

She motioned the girl who trotted off, then came back, telling Hortense: "She says that will be fine."

I got home around five, and at once tried to call Teddy. I found out from Miss Nettie that she'd been calling me, on my own phone and through the switchboard. When at last I got hold of her, she piled right in, asking me what was up, what Hortense wanted. I told her I didn't know, but it might be about what Garrett

253

would have put in his will if he'd lived long enough to make one. "Not to string it out," I said, "you fix up your face so it's pretty, especially how it looks with a smile, and be nice to this dame, nice as you know how to be. Because, get this, Teddy, he made notes for a will which Sam Dent was to be guided by in drawing it up. But he did not make a will. Sam never got that far. He was looking over the notes, to know how to draw the will up, when Inga got in the act, and that rang down the curtain. *But*, it may very well be, and there's reason to think it is, that she feels she must do what he wanted—what Mr. Garrett wanted, I mean—and that's what's on her mind with this invitation to you. It may be she means to act snotty and tell you she's sorry she can't, or won't, or is not going to pay you the money. But knowing her and how she feels about things, I would say it's just the opposite. She means to pay over what he wanted you to have so she can have peace of mind. But for some reason she wants to talk or say something to you or whatever. She's been awfully ill, and ill people do strange things. But from where you sit, a grin on your face may mean the difference between cutting in on the sugar and not cutting in on it. Do you hear what I say, Teddy?"

"Yes, Dr. Palmer, of course."

"What do you say?"

"I say O.K."

"There's to be no saucy talk. Do you promise?"

"Before I say, *you* say. How much is in it for me?"

"Plenty. He was no piker, Teddy."

"You mean like six-figure dough?"

"At least that."

"Then I won't blow it. Wild horses couldn't make me."

254

"Then, O.K. Love you."

"Likewise. Double."

The next day when I arrived, a full house was already there—Sam, the secretary Winifred, the nurse with no name, the baby, and Mrs. Mendenhall. And Hortense—still stretched out in her chair and still looking pale, wan, and tragic. I bowed, then took a chair at one side and waited. We all waited, saying nothing. But this time, instead of making a row, I sat there, going along. I suppose a half-hour went by before the buzzer sounded, and Winifred took it. "Send her up," she said and in a moment went out in the hall. Then Teddy made her entrance, and it *was* an entrance.

She had on the mink coat, with beige trousers showing below it, a dark crimson band on her hair, and crimson shoes. With her dark hair and black eyes, she was very Spanish-looking, which seems to include a dangerous cut to the jib. I mean, I thought of all the dancers I had ever heard of, that by the look in their eye would just as soon knife you as kiss you. She was nice as pie to Hortense, however, making a little curtsey to her and saying: "So nice to see you again," and then turning with a smile to the others, seeming to know them all except for the nurse. Hortense asked her to sit down, then began: "Miss Rodriguez, my husband, before he died, wrote up notes for his will, which he didn't live to sign. But naturally, I feel I should carry out his wishes whether he made legal provision or not—which is why I asked you to come. It was his intention, Miss Rodriguez, to leave you a million dollars."

"Hey! He did things big, didn't he?"

"However, I feel I must make a condition."

"What?"

"The day of the press conference, Miss Rodreguez, I missed the performance you gave, so before handing over this check that I've drawn for you"—she got an evelope from her bag and flipped it around in her hand—"I was wondering if you'd be kind enough to repeat it for me here now today?"

Teddy stood there, swallowed two or three times, and at last drew a long breath. "Mrs. Garrett," she half-whispered, "how'd you like to go to hell?"

"Teddy!" I said. "What about those wild horses!"

"Very well, I'll forget the check."

Hortense dropped it back in her bag. "Goddamn it," I roared at Teddy, "take it back, apologize! So she tried to pee on you. So you knew she was going to, but for one million bucks you can buy enough Listerine to deoderize all the pee ever peed, and if you've got any brains, *you'll apologize. Now!*"

"Then, Mrs. Garrett, I take it back; I'm sorry."

"Very well. This exhibition can proceed."

"It began with a walkover. It's kind of like a bow."

"A very nice start, I would say."

Teddy took off her coat and pitched it on a chair. Then she put her hands on the floor, lifted one leg behind her, let it drop over her head, lifted the other leg, let the first leg touch in front, and while the other leg was flipping down, pushed up with her hands to come standing again. "Very nicely done," said Hortense. "I applaud."

She patted her fingertips together, and Teddy went on: "Next off, for the reporters, I did a handstand facing them, on account of one dame said that a earth-shaking thing had not been invented yet, to get my front end where my face was and my hind end where my patches were, in the same shot at the same time. This way—"

She repeated that handstand she had done that other time, and Hortense gravely told her: "Beautifully done. I applaud one more time."

"Thank you, Mrs. Garrett."

She stood there a moment, then went on: "Then, of course, there were the handstands I did for your husband."

"I beg your pardon?"

"Oh, I knew him quite well, Mrs. Garrett."

"I didn't realize you did handstands for him."

"All the time. The idea was that he get inspired to do unto me that which I hoped for always. It didn't work out that way, as he was under a thrall, he called it. I still don't quite know what a thrall is. I think it's some kind of hex that a woman had on him. At the time I suspected that the Swede was the one who plugged him. I must have been right. Mrs. Garrett, I hope I didn't upset you?"

"It's quite all right. Go on."

"If I did get out of line, I'm sorry—"

"She said go on," I told her.

"Yeah, I'd do handstands for him and then walk on my hands, past him—always without any clothes on. And as I went by, I'd drop one leg forward and the other leg behind, for the upside-down split, which he liked. This way—but first I've got to take off some clothes."

She started to unbutton her blouse, but Hortense beat her to it. "No!" she exclaimed, in a half-hysterical voice. "I get the idea."

"Well, I don't mind, Mrs. Garrett."

"I do."

257

"So," I said, taking my position in front of Hortense, "you thought it was going to be fun, peeing on Teddy Rodriguez, and then she peed on you—"

"What do you mean, using such language to me?"

"If my language offends you, I apologize. I withdraw pee. She *pissed* on you, I should say, and that takes care of her. It doesn't take care of me. I have things to say—"

"You have nothing to say. You may go."

"I'm going—don't worry, I'm not enjoying myself any more than you are. But there's somebody here who concerns me—a beautiful little boy who's as much mine as yours. That boy I mean to have, and if you don't surrender him now, I mean to claim him in court. I'm going to have you declared an unfit mother—"

"Dr. Palmer, are you insane?"

"Not that I know of. You don't want this child. You don't care about him. You've had him a month now, and haven't even given him a name. That makes you unfit, as I'll damned convince the court. But to take custody of a child, I have to have a wife who can act as a mother to him. As my wife, I mean to take Teddy—"

"Hey, hey, not so fast!"

That was Teddy who jumped up and said: "I've got something to say about that. Nobody's marrying me as a way of getting a child. I have to be loved for myself alone—"

"You'll be loved enough; don't worry."

"On that basis, I accept."

"Dr. Palmer," Hortense said, a vicious look in her eye, "I hope you take me to court. To prove you're the father of this boy, you'll have to admit that you blackmailed a woman, that you touched her husband for money, that you seduced his wife, that you lied to him. And just how fit the court will think you, to take custody of a child, even with Teddy's help, I wouldn't like to say. Please feel free to sue, if that's what it's called. It'll be your word against mine, and if I deny— as I will—that you are the child's father, I doubt very much that the court will believe you. A man may think he knows who the child's father is, but a woman *knows* she knows."

"Sometime, if you give your sworn word to the court about something that's not true, you'll do a stretch for perjury. That's one thing a court won't accept. When I point out that this boy has the same double mole on his throat as I have on mine, any judge on earth will know who's telling the truth."

"Get out of here! All of you!"

Everyone shuffled their feet. Nobody moved.

For some time the air was thick. All you could hear was Hortense's sobs. Then the baby got into the act, with a sudden, furious squall that was tiny and at the same time so piercing it stabbed at your ears. The nurse took a bottle from the table, tried the nipple with her finger, and put it down in the crib against the baby's mouth. "He's not hungry," Teddy said.

"You know if he's hungry or not?" snarled Hortense.

"Yes, I know. Why don't you?"

She was very cold. The nurse kept pushing the nipple at the baby's mouth, but the squawling kept right on. Then she began shaking the crib. Teddy went over, took her by the wrist exactly as she'd taken Hortense the day of the press conference, and began backing her up, just as she'd backed Hortense. Then she flung her into a chair and turned to the baby who was still hooking it, sucking in deep breaths, then stiffening with a jerk and letting go. She picked him up, carried him back to her chair, and sat down—but holding his head with one hand in such way as to support it, and bending her face toward his.

"Little sweetheart," she crooned at him, "has a mother that's hipped on dough, the millions she has in the bank, grandmother hipped on booze, and a nurse that thinks he's a butter churn—when all he wanted was *love!*" She breathed this in his face, and suddenly the squawling dropped off, to surprised little gasps, one after the other. Then he *laughed.* If there's anything so beautiful as the sudden, gurgling laugh of a little child, I wouldn't know what it is. I sat there with my throat playing me tricks, gulping and gagging and swallowing. I wasn't looking at Hortense, and didn't until I heard something, but then I did look and saw she was doing what I was trying not to do—sobbing, her chin on her chest, the tears pouring down her cheeks. Suddenly she waved her hand in a way that meant only one thing: leave me alone, go. Mrs. Mendenhall tiptoed out, followed by Sam, the nurse, and Winifred. But when Teddy got up, Hortense made opposite motions, beckoning her over, holding out her arms for the boy. Teddy, first kneeling beside her, gave him to her, carefully cuddling his head on Hortense's shoulder. It left Hortense with one free hand, and she grabbed Teddy's hand, raising it to her lips and kissing it.

"May I called you Teddy?" she whispered.

"Please. I want you to."

"Teddy, you've given me back my soul."

29

Then we all three gave way to tears, and for some moments let them come, not even trying to hold them back. And once more, the baby got in the act, starting to bawl again, but in such a comical way that we had to laugh. Then we were laughing and crying at the same time, and Hortense was talking to him, sweet, low, and mumbly, the way a mother should. Pretty soon she turned to Teddy who was still kneeling beside her and told her: "It's true what he said, Dr. Palmer—until now, I hadn't chosen a name for him. I didn't care. He didn't seem real to me. They told me he was mine, that he'd been taken from me, but to me he was nothing. Now, thanks to you, Teddy, he's not. You uttered the one word, love, that changed everything, and rebuked me, and chastened me, and woke me. Teddy, will you be my child's godmother? Will you let me name him for you? My I call him Theodore?"

"Oh, Mrs. Garrett, I'd feel so *honored!*"

"Teddy, to you from now on, I'm Hortense."

"Mrs. Garrett, I wouldn't quite have the nerve."

"Since when are you so shy?"

I meant it to be funny, but it snapped out just the

least bit short, and she jumped up, facing me, as though to bat me one in the jaw. Then we all laughed. "Getting back to the main point," Hortense said, "as soon as I'm able, to have him baptized—"

"You're going to ask me, Mrs. Garrett?"

"You can hold him. And if Lloyd would like to come—?"

It caught my ear as an odd kind of remark and seemed to catch Teddy's, too.

"What did you say, Mrs. Garrett? Why wouldn't Dr. Palmer like to come?"

"Well, if you and he are getting married—?"

"*Are you being funny, or what?*"

"Well, he said he was marrying you, and you said—"

"That's right, I shot off my mouth quite a lot, but that was before I give you back your soul—"

"*Gave* her back her soul," I corrected.

"That's what I said. Stop hacking at me. Mrs. Garrett, now that you've got back your soul, I think Dr. Palmer loves you."

"Teddy, he also loves you."

"Maybe, but not as much and not in the right way."

"There's only one way to love."

"*Goddamn it, do you want this guy or don't you?*"

Teddy ripped it out, then suddenly burst into tears. Once more, we all were crying, and this time when the baby got in it, he really meant business. We got ourselves under control, and for several minutes Hortense whispered to him. Then once more he calmed down and sat, all three of us staring at nothing, not looking at each other.

Suddenly Hortense turned to me with a mean look in

her eye. "So," she snapped, "Teddy's spoken her piece, and I've spoken mine. But you've said nothing at all. What *do* you say, Lloyd?"

"On the subject of marriage, you mean?"

"It's the subject we're on, isn't it?"

"I don't say anything, until you say more than you have. Since that night in College Park, since that night when you just disappeared, you've not been the same to me. That I know of, I've done nothing to you. So before I say anything, you can. What have I done to you? What's it all about, the way you've been treating me?"

"You haven't done anything."

It was some moments before she said it, and there seemed to be more coming. I waited, and she went on: "That's right—I left you, left your bed, left your place in College Park with a beautiful scheme I had, to be Little Miss Fixit, so you and I could be married, so I could be yours, and you at last would be mine. And my scheme blew up in my face. I have my pride, I guess. You didn't do anything, that I repeat again— but I can't look at you. I can't look you in the eye!"

"But where does *my* eye come in?"

"Are you deaf? It was you I wanted to marry!"

"Well, do you still?"

"What do you think? What do you—"

But with that she completely collapsed. Teddy jumped up, went over, and took the baby again. But it didn't start to cry. In her arms it looked up and laughed. I went over and patted Hortense, first on the arm, then on the cheek.

"Look at me," I told her.

At last, she did.

"I'm taking you home."

Her eyes closed, she smiled, and then motioned Teddy to give her back the child. "Little Theodore," she whispered. "Such a beautiful name."

She smiled down on him while Teddy stood on one side of her chair and I on the other. Then suddenly she started to talk briskly and businesslike. "As soon as we decently can, we'll be married, of course. Until then, he has to be Theodore Garrett—using Lloyd's name at this state would simply blight his life. Books have been written about it, the torture people go through once rumors get around about their legitimacy. But then, when we're married, Lloyd can adopt him, and then things will be in line. There'll be no trouble about it. It happens all the time, that when someone marries a woman who has a child, he adopts it and then it uses his name. But until then—"

"Until when?" asked Teddy.

"Until we get married, Teddy."

"Why don't you get married today?"

"Well, there's a matter of the license—and the waiting period—and a decent interval, after all that happened—"

"Decent? For who?"

"Whom," I said.

But Teddy paid no attention. "For the eye of the law, there's a waiting period, but in the eye of God, there needn't be. It was explained by the priest when my father married again after my mother died, and before my sister came, that I babysat for so much. He told my father: 'It's not me who performs this marriage—I pronounce it performed, and file a certificate of it. But you two marry each other.' He then repeated the words of the service, 'With this ring, I thee wed,'

264

and so forth and so on, which thrilled me, just listening to it. So I learned it up by heart, how it goes at that point, and can lead you through it right now, if you'd like me to do it—"

"Well, if we just had a ring—"

"So happens, we do have a ring."

I took the ring out of my wallet. It was wrapped in its chamois cover. "It was my mother's," I said. "The undertaker took it from her finger and gave it to me at the funeral. It's been with me ever since—and she would want you to wear it."

I offered it to Hortense, and after staring at it, she said: "I feel thrilled. Teddy, if you really want to take charge—"

"I want to pray first."

She disappeared into the dining room.

"There's one thing, Lloyd," Hortense said. "You haven't answered me yet, on ARMALCO—"

"You mean, on my being president of it?"

"Yes—so I can have some peace."

"Then if you want me as president, all right."

"And one other thing: I want you to tape it—our story so I can type it up. I want you to put it all in—every kiss, every crazy remark. Then we can read it on anniversaries and relive our beautiful romance. And *he*, when he's old enough, can read it and learn *why* he was adopted and *why* he must use your name."

"Then, consider it done."

At that moment, I knew she was still my Hortense, popping from a hundred-million-dollar decision to a romance pure and simple. Then Teddy was back. She took our hands and put them inside each other, biting her lips just a little. "God has given me peace," she said. "Please repeat after me, Lloyd. Now, at last, I must call you that—'I, Lloyd, take thee, Hortense'—now, at last, I call you that—'to be my wedded wife—' "

It lasted no more than a minute, and I felt proud and decent and holy as I slipped the ring on Hortense's finger, our child still in her arms. Then I kissed her. Then I kissed Teddy. Then she kissed Hortense, said "Goodbye, good luck, God bless"—and suddenly was gone.

"I want to go home," Hortense said.

"You mean, to College Park?"

"It's where my home is usually found."

"Fine, I love it. But where we put *him* I don't know. That is, if we're taking him. There's no place out there he can—"

"Of course we're taking him! And where we put him is in his crib. It comes apart, and the porter will take it down to your car."

"*I'll* take it down to my car."

"Then, will you hold him while I unhook it?"

She held him to me, blowing into his neck and whispering "Little Theodore." Then I was holding this tiny, this incredibly tiny thing, in my arms. It opened its eyes and smiled. "Oh!" she yelped. "He's looking at you!"

"Well, why not? Am I repulsive or something?"

"But until now, his eyes haven't focussed!"

"They got something to focus *on!*"

"You crazy goof!"

I guess that covers it. I'm taped up.

ABOUT THE AUTHOR . . .

A writer of tremendous vitality, James M. Cain gained fame during the 1930's with his short, pithy crime novels, including *The Postman Always Rings Twice* and *Double Indemnity*. He was compared favorably with Dashiell Hammett and Raymond Chandler, and shared honors with Hemingway as the most honored, most widely read American author.

Since then his literary reputation has had its ups and downs, but his new books were always good sellers and reprints of his earlier works enjoyed consistent popularity. After his death in 1977, a new groundswell of enthusiasm has led to the reprinting of many of his books. Several different companies have recently published or are planning to bring out various collections of his work in special editions. Among these books are both the most famous ones, such as *The Postman Always Rings Twice*, *Double Indemnity*, *Serenade* and *Mildred Pierce*, and the less well-known ones that are not being rediscovered, such as *The Institute*, the last book Cain wrote.

Starting as a newspaperman, Cain had a natural instinct for relating the story behind the headlines in the kind of crimes featured in the tabloids. Not that his books are simply fictionalized news stories; they are his own inventions, though occasionally suggested by real-life happenings. Thus his first novel, *Postman*, owes some of its inspiration to the famous Ruth Snyder-Judd Gray murder trial. *Rainbow's End*, which is more reminiscent of Cain's early high-speed, punchy writing style than his other recent books, was suggested by the D. B. Cooper skyjacking case.

What distinguishes Cain's novels from the average quickly-forgotten thriller is the breathless drive of his writing and also its very individualistic moral and philosophical slant. The fact is that Cain himself bore little resemblance to his passion-driven, morally confused characters. The son of a college president, trained by the distinguished language stylists H. L. Mencken and Walter Lippmann, he was slow in realizing where his own particular talents as an author lay. It was Lippmann who convinced a publisher to accept *Postman*, his first book, when Cain was 42 years old. But once started, he was hard to stop. He died with pen in hand, so to speak, at the age of 84, soon after his eighteenth novel was published.

Cain's graphic style has always attracted filmmakers. Fourteen of his novels have appeared as motion pictures or television shows; some have been filmed several times. The latest to become a movie project is *Past All Dishonor*, one of his recent books and one of the few with a historical (Civil War) background.

THE REAPING

An ancient superstition reaches out, catching you in a net of horror and suspense

The Reaping

LEISURE
1835
$2.50

BERNARD TAYLOR

"Taylor works wizardry again here."
—PUBLISHERS WEEKLY

He was hired to paint the portrait of a young woman at Woolvercombe Mansion, but Tom Rigby didn't know she was after more than a painting. He wondered about the identities of the strange inhabitants of the house and the bizarre events that began to happen. And suddenly he was catapulted into a rendezvous with terror and violence, as the power of the supernatural wielded its horrifying spell!

By Bernard Taylor

CATEGORY:
Occult
PRICE: $2.50
0-8439-1035-6

EXPENSIVE PLEASURES
By Stephen Lewis

PRICE: $2.95

LB929

CATEGORY: Novel

WHAT HAPPENS WHEN A WOMAN'S *EVERY* FANTASY COMES TRUE?

Cara fulfilled her wildest dreams as a superstar model. But she wanted more, and indulged in one more fantasy—to succeed as a fashion designer. Her inspired designs and transcontinental romances carried her to the apex of the fashion industry and high society. But behind her public smile hid the private pain of lovers lost in a world of diamond-studded decadence, sexual abandon, and betrayal. Soon, everyone wore her designer jeans and envied her extravagant lifestyle. But would all her fantasies come true? Would the high risks be worth those EXPENSIVE PLEASURES....A sizzling novel from the author of THE REGULARS and THE BEST SELLERS.

Marguerite had struck a bargain with life, trading her beauty, her only asset, for security. Now she had achieved the goals she had set for herself as a penniless young girl — wealth, position, a successful husband, attractive children. Then dynamic Lou Armitage entered her life. Consumed by a passion she could not control, Marguerite willingly risked the destruction of the very world she had so carefully constructed!

By Elizabeth Dubus

PRICE: $2.95
0-8439-1037-2
CATEGORY:
Novel

SEND TO: **LEISURE BOOKS**
P.O. Box 511, Murry Hill Station
New York, N.Y. 10156-0511

Please send the titles:

Quantity	Book Number	Price
————	————————	————
————	————————	————
————	————————	————
————	————————	————
————	————————	————

In the event we are out of stock on any of your
selections, please list alternate titles below.

————	————————	————
————	————————	————
————	————————	————
————	————————	————

Postage/Handling ————

I enclose ————

FOR U.S. ORDERS, add 75¢ for the first book and 25¢ for
each additional book to cover cost of postage and handling.
Buy five or more copies and we will pay for shipping. Sorry,
no. C.O.D.'s.

FOR ORDERS SENT OUTSIDE THE U.S.A., add $1.00
for the first book and 50¢ for each additional book. PAY BY
foreign draft or money order drawn on a U.S. bank, payable
in U.S. ($) dollars.

☐ Please send me a free catalog.

NAME _____

(Please print)

ADDRESS _____

CITY ————STATE ————ZIP————

Allow Four Weeks for Delivery